GUNZ -N- BUTTER

The Code for the Streets

BY
DEYON LEE

So You Can Write Publications[TM]
P.O. Box 80736
Milwaukee, WI 53208
Phone: (920)-821-3006

Library of Congress Cataloging-in-Publication Data

Lee, Deyon
GUNZ -N- BUTTER: The Code for the Streets
Published by So You Can Write Publications, LLC
8/15/2025

www.sycwp.com
home4writers@sycwp.com

ISBN: 979-8-9899762-6-3 (sc)

SO YOU CAN WRITE
PUBLICATIONS®

Dedication

**In loving memory
of
Bertha Louise Lee**

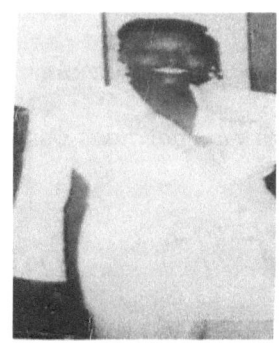

Chapter 1

Butter sat at the table in the kitchen at his downtown Milwaukee condominium with two money counting machines. He was counting the money from his drug sales from the last few months. His first in command street soldier Brick, was with him getting the money ready to take to his plug. It was seven days away from being July 6th, the day his dawg Double P, b.k.a DP was getting released from prison after doing *10* years for a drug case. Butter has been waiting for this day since DP went to jail for the dope case that was meant for him. DP took Butter's case because he was the one who put Butter in the drug game at a young age. Butter had everything planned for his mentor, and he wanted everything to go right for the homecoming of DP da big homie.

"Brick, the nicca I was telling you about is about to touchdown like a football game. In *5* days and a muthafucking wake up, ya hear me? Fool the streets ain't ready for what's about to take place. My nicca, this shit is about to go da fuck down! Consider yourself lucky because you're about to be a part of fucking dope boy history my boy!" Butter told Brick as he put the last of the drug money in the 3rd Gucci bag and tossed it in the corner of the kitchen where two more bags were full of money. Brick was from New York and had been living in Milwaukee for the last years with his grandmother. At the age of 21 Brick was 6'4 and 220 lbs solid.

Butter hooked up with Brick when he was *17*. Brick met Butter two months after he moved to Milwaukee and

5

was working at the car wash Octopus on Green Bay Road. Butter had seen Brick slap the shit out of somebody who accused him of stealing change out of his car. The owner of Octopus fired Brick right there on the spot. So, in return Brick turned around and slapped the shit out of him also before tearing off his work apron and walking out of the car wash. Butter saw that Brick was a young nicca who had some potential and knew with the right guidance Brick would be a loyal street soldier.

"Aye Butter you know I'm with cha to the end. You showed me getting this paper is easy, so you know I'd never bite the hand that fed me," the loyal street soldier said, while grabbing the two money counting machines off the marble table and setting them in the cabinet over the sink. Where Butter also kept three scales and two .45 guns with extra clips.

"Aye lil homie, you know I know the real you. So, what's understood doesn't need to be explained," Butter told Brick.

"So, boss what all you got planned for the release of your dawg Double P?"

"You know Brick, it's gonna be one to remember. This muthafucker 'DP' showed me the game, gave me and taught me the game. Plus, the stretch he just did was all because I fucked up," Butter said, while rolling up a blunt of Purple Haze.

"So, Butter you telling me that the nicca who is getting out of Waupun Prison next week is in there because of you?" Brick asked, while tossing his Green Bay Packer's Bic lighter to Butter, so he could dry the diamond White Owl blunt he just rolled up full of that purple haze.

"Yeah, my nicca, it was *10* years ago DP and I was chilling at this dope spot he had on 2nd and Wright. DP knew the trap was about to get hit by the people, at any day. And made it a point not to keep any drugs of any kind there," Butter told the story while passing the perfect rolled blunt to Brick, who took a strong pull and started coughing up his insides.

"Damn my nicca, you rolled the shit out of this shit. This muthafucker hitting harder than 'Tyson'."

"I know nicca I rolled that dope, take notes cause my nicca your blunts don't be hitting worth shit," Butter said, as he laughed at Brick who's eyes began to water.

"Whatever son, just finish the story B." Brick had been in Milwaukee going on almost 5 years and his New York accent was still pretty noticeable.

"Anyway Brick, I was chilling in the trap with this little hoe. Me and the chick were smoking and drinking, you know, doing us, right?" Butter paused long enough to accept his perfectly rolled blunt back from Brick. Butter inhaled deeply then tilted his head up towards the ceiling fan before blowing out the thick purple smoke before continuing. The ceiling fan cut through the smoke like a helicopter cutting through on a dark gloomy day. "So, as me and Shorty started kissing and grinding our hands touching each other everywhere and shit."

Brick stopped Butter right in the middle of his story. "Hold up, hold up kid, you trying to tell me you were in a lip lock with Shorty?" Brick asked, with a childish grin on his face.

"Damn fool, do you wanna hear this shit or not?" Butter snapped with an irritated tone in his voice.

"Yeah, you right kid, please continue," Brick said, while getting up to plug his Galaxy 27 phone on the charger in the living room.

Butter followed his most trusted soldier into the living room and flopped down on his *$5,000*-dollar leather sectional couch before finishing. "But like I was saying before I was rudely interrupted. Me and this lil chick are doing our thang, while the big homie is knocked out sleeping in the backroom. My nicca, next thing I know the muthafucking pigs was kicking down the fucking door. Throwing me and the chick on the floor and dragging DP out the backroom!" Butter said while passing the almost gone purple haze blunt to Brick.

"Damn kid, you might as well finish this joint," Brick said before hitting the cigar two more times before putting it out in the ashtray that was next to his charging cell phone.

"Nicca if you want more, it's a pound in the back, roll up and shut the fuck up, nicca. I'm trying to tell you the story."

"Alright son, your world," Brick said.

"Ok, like I was saying, the pigs got all three of us laid out on the living room floor. I'm sweating, the bitch is crying and I looked over to see the boy DP with a big ass crest toothpaste smile on his face. 20 minutes later the cops are holding *9* ounces of crack over our head."

"Damn son," Brick said.

"You telling me G," Butter replied. "Anyway, long story short, DP took my weight and the only thing I could do was put my head down into the carpet. Because I was supposed to have taken that shit to the other spot. DP told them pink people it was his dope and to call his lawyer. That was *10* years ago and my nicca wouldn't ever have been in prison, if I didn't see that chick who I had in the spot. Because I would've taken that dope where it was supposed to go."

8

"Yeah son, it sounds like you're a true soldier. I can't wait to make my peace with God." Brick told Butter, while walking towards the back to grab some of that purple haze to roll up.

Butter sat there on the couch lost in his thoughts about the return of DP, when he went to prison Butter was just a youngin trying to make a buck. The day after DP went to jail, Butter went to his 2nd trap house and discovered a brick of cocaine and *$30,000* dollars. Once he heard from his mentor, Butter was to give the *$30,000* to DP's lawyer and told the whereabouts of two more Kilos and to make it do what it does, with three kilos. And when he needed more, to buy them from the lawyer. Within those *10* years Butter and the lawyer Mr. Kirk has done a lot of business, making them both really rich men. Butter was brought out of his thoughts by the ringing of Brick's cell phone.

"Ring, Ring…."

Butter looked at the screen of the phone and saw it was Ecstasy, the only female in his crew.

"Say Brick, it's Ecstasy hitting yo line."

Brick came out of the backroom with an extended blunt between his hands. "Yo kid answer the phone for shorty while I rolled this piece here," Brick said as he sat on the opposite side of the sectional.

Butter grabbed Brick's cell off the glass diamond shaped coffee table and unplugged it from the charger. "Ecstasy wuz sup baby girl.?"

"Who is this Butter?" Ecstasy asked.

"You know this, tell me something good Ma." Butter told Ecstasy.

"Well Butter, two of the traps are out and the house on South Rogers is low. So, tell that New York ass nicca to get on it with his bullshitting ass," Ecstasy said, before she hung up the phone. Butter looked at the phone then at Brick.

Brick caught the look Butter had on his face. "What kid, shorty popped off didn't she?"

Butter kind of had a feeling that Brick and Ecstasy was messing around. He really didn't care as long as it didn't interfere with his money. "Yeah, she did it, I don't know what y'all two got going on as long as you remember cash then ass last, big homie. But let's get ready to vacate my nicca. Because one thing she did say was that at least three of the traps are out," Butter said while raising up off the couch and snatching his car keys off the diamond shaped table all in one motion.

Brick walked back into the kitchen to grab his Packer Bic lighter off the marble table. "Right behind you kid and don't worry about me and shorty. I'm gonna get that under control. The only thing you need to be concerned about is getting things right for that kid DP and not hitting this blunt too hard." Brick told Butter as he closed the door as they walked to the elevator on their floor.

They took the elevator to the underground garage where Brick's midnight blue Q7 was parked. Once inside the truck, Brick pulled out his nickel plated .45 pistol that he always kept on his waistline and set it on his lap. "Ok God, where to go first?" Brick asked.

"So do you need a piece to go see the owner of that club 'Rain' for the big party you are having there?" Butter asked while push starting the Audi truck. When the truck pulled out of the underground garage it looked like the earth opened up and spit out one of the finest trucks made. With 26-inch custom chrome Forge's and $3,500-dollar sound system. Brick had the city of Milwaukee on lock far as Audi goes. Just to piss off the haters, he had three TV's, two in the headrest of the seats and one in the dashboard; along with **Brick Seven** piped in the front and back seats.

Butter asked him what Brick Seven meant one day and he just turned to him and said, "After I'm dead, I'll continue to shit on these niccas 7 times over."

"You know what Brick, that's a good idea. Swing by that joint 'Rain' so I can make sure everything gonna be set up for DP big bash, Mr. Seven."

When Brick pulled into the parking lot of the club Rain, there were only a few cars there, but even if the lot was full nobody could miss the owner's pearl white Bentley truck sitting on some nice 24-inch Bentley rims. It was five o'clock in the evening and club Rain had a nice semi crowd due to the fact the back of the club was used for gambling for the real big ballers of the city. At the door of Rain, Butter and Brick was greeted by the head of security Big Vest. Now Big Vest was 6'7 and 325 lbs. He got his name because he was shot in the chest 6 times and still refuses to wear a vest.

"What up Butter and Brick, y'all here to see Ms. Shelly I presume?"

"Yeah, that's right. You tell Ms. Boss lady, I am here," Butter said while dropping the Kool's cigarette he was smoking on the ground and crushing it out with his Gucci Loafer.

"I got you Butter, y'all have a seat at the bar and I'll get Ms. Shelly out the back."

Chapter 2

Ms. Shelly was one of the few females to hold her own and make it out of the Milwaukee ghetto streets. Being that her big brother was heavy in the streets, the baby sister didn't give her a pass. After he went to prison for a life sentence, Shelly took over the crew he had started and with his instruction from the inside Shelly ran his crew with an iron fist. As soon as she got her money up Shelly opened up the clubs Rain and the strip club US, two of the biggest clubs Milwaukee had seen in years. She was making so much money off the clubs alone, Shelly left the streets to the street punks and became a straight and legit business woman.

The crew that she ran, with the help of her brother, she left to the next runner up who promised her, once she was out, she was out for life and wasn't coming back or asking for help if some old drama came her way. Shelly wasn't worried at all because when she was in the streets, Shelly killed better than some men. She gained her respect and rank in the streets by killing or giving the okay to kill some of Milwaukee's most feared gangsters. To look at it, one would never guess her hands had so much blood on them.

Shelly was 38 years young, her skin color was mocha brown and she wore her hair in a wild nappy afro; she also had dimples that will put Lauren London to shame. Shelly stood a 5'10 with measurements of 32-24-36. She was the true definition of a real stallion. When Shelly decided to go legit she brought along her closest friend and security Big Vest. Big Vest has been watching over Shelly since she was a little girl and her big brother went to the pen. Big Vest and Shelly's brother have been road dawgs since they were little. They even started their crew together, but when Shelly's big brother got his murder rap, Big Vest only wanted to play the back field to the crew and go unnoticed. Because he was supposed to be doing life with Shelly's brother.

Shelly was lost deep in her thoughts when she heard a knock on her office door. "Knock, Knock."

"Yes, come on in Vest."

"Sorry to disturb you boss lady, but that youngster Butter is here to see you."

Shelly looked at the fire department calendar on her wall to check what date and month it was. "Ok, Vest please show them in, thank you."

When Big Vest made it back out to the bar he saw Butter at the bar sipping on an MGD and his man Brick at a table conversing with two females that came in early for a few cocktails. "Ok, Butter, boss lady will see you now, no disrespect but you know how this shit go." Big Vest told Butter.

"Yeah, big guy I know the drill." Butter told him as he stood up to let Big Vest pat him down. Brick started to rise when he saw a big dude patting down his boss. Butter saw him out of the corner of his eye. "Chill. Brick, continue to do yo thang with them ladies. Imma go holler at Shelly for a second and I'll be right back." Butter told his most loyal soldier.

For one, he knew that Shelly was ok with people and it was all about money with her, and for two, Butter knew it would've been a whole big thing between Brick and Big Vest because Brick wasn't about to give up his pistol. Big

Vest escorted him to the back of the club where they came to this back door. Big Vest gave the door two knocks when Butter heard the voice of Shelly.

"Come in Butter."

Butter walked into a bar office that looked better than some people's living room. Shelly had a fish tank that was made inside the wall that was occupied by some vicious looking piranhas, she also had a TV that was mounted on the wall that showed every angle inside and outside of the bar and parking lot. Her office desk was two desks in one, which was made out of marble.

Shelly and Big Vest were the only two people that knew Shelly had a *12*-gauge strap to the inside of her desk in case one of her business meetings went wrong. Butter set in the leather king size recliner chair that sat in front of Shelly's desk and *12*-gauge. Once he was seated Shelly excused Big Vest.

"Okay, boss lady, I'll be out front if you need me." Was all the big security-brother said before closing the door.

"Damn Shelly, this here is a fucking nice office, and this goddamn chair I'm sitting in fit my ass like a glove," Butter said.

"Glad you like it Butter, but I'm pretty sure you're not here to check out your ass in my *$3,000*-dollar chair, so let's get down to business."

Butter pulled out his pack of Kools cigarettes. "Yeah Shelly you're right, do you mind if I smoke?"

"Not at all Butter."

He took out his lighter and lit his cigarette. "Ok, Shelly, I want to rent out this club and the V.I.P section next Friday for the homecoming of my big homie DP. So how much?"

Shelly remembers hearing the name DP for being a major hitter back in the days but didn't know him. "Butter, hit me with *$10,000* and I'll make sure your boy has the homecoming of his life. None stop bottles of your choice, women of all flavors. Plus, I can have Boosie Badass perform that night and do a walkthrough in V.I.P since he's gonna be in town.

"Yeah, Shelly, that sounds like a plan." Butter set the Kool cigarette he was smoking in the ashtray sitting on Shelly's desk.

Then he went into his pants and brought out a wad of hundred-dollar bills and tossed it on her desk. "That's eleven bands Shelly, you can keep the change and sorry if it's dirty seeing that it was in my boxers and all," Butter said with a smile on his face as he grabbed his Kool cigarette back out of the ashtray.

Shelly grabbed the wad of money in her well-manicured hands off her desk. "Butter, just make sure you and your boys show my club some respect. And about this money," Shelly put the *$11,000* dollars in her bra. "I had dirtier money. You can see yourself out Butter."

When Butter made it back to the front of the club, he saw Brick in a lip lock with both chicks he was sitting at the table with. "Let's bounce, lover boy," he said to Brick as he passed him on his way to the front door. Brick got right up to follow his boss. He told the two chicks to meet him at the club next Friday and drinks were on him as he walked out the front door.

Shelly sat at her desk and watched Butter and Brick pull out of the parking lot before she went back to the stack of business papers on her desk.

Chapter 3

It was rec time at Waupun Max Correctional Prison and the only person who was walking the track was inmate #306278 B.K.A. DP. The only reason DP was the only person on track is because it was a fall time out and it was pouring down raining. DP didn't really care about the rain. After 10 years he was getting ready to get released back into the community and was trying to get his mind right. When DP first came to prison he caught a battery charge in Dodge intake prison that landed him in Waupun Max. Where for the first four years DP kept up his violent rage temper on any and everybody. Until one day he was released from solitary confinement after doing a year from beating his old cellmate so badly that the inmate had to stay in the infirmary for two months.

That's when he got celled up with a lifer that went by the name of FP. Now FP was doing a life bit for running one of the most feared crews in the whole state of Wisconsin called the T-Y-L crew. DP had heard about the Take Your Life crew and FP when he started doing his things in the streets of Milwaukee. DP remembers the day he was released out the hole and celled up with FP. As soon as DP laid his things on the top bunk FP stepped into the room.

"Say little brother, since you came into this prison, I've been keeping watch on you."

DP stopped what he was doing and turned to FP. "Check FP, I know about you and your T-Y-L crew. Why you peeping me out? I don't know, but one thing I do know is that I ain't going for no punking or hoeing. So, you can get that shit out of your thinking box, Killa." DP was ready for whatever FP was about to throw his way.

At this time, DP wasn't that heavy on the weight size but he could throw with the best of them. He sat there staring FP dead in the eyes and was wondering why this lifer had this goofy smile on his face.

"Dp relax my nicca. I don't swing that way, plus if I wanted you touched, I could've gotten you murked last week in the chow hall, where I had that sucka as guard Mr. Sabourin taken out of his misery for fucking up my pipeline for cigarettes." Right at that moment FP pulled out a pack of Newport Kings. "Here you go. DP take a smoke and let's rap." DP looked at FP like he was fucking crazy.

"No disrespect captain but you just had a guard wacked for fucking up your cigarettes pipe line. Now you're here offering me a Newport. Now playboy I think I'll pass on the smoke but I would like to know why you've been clocking me out of all the niccas in this joint?"

"Fuck it DP, if you don't want to smoke I ain't gonna beg you my nicca but I will tell you why I been checking out your swag since day one. You know the streets talk and for a nicca like me, I'm the one the streets talk to and about."

"Meaning what?" Dp asked, still trying to figure out what FP was on.

"Meaning, I know about you. I know that you're doing a dime right now because your youngin fucked up by keeping the dope at the wrong trap. And instead of letting him take the rap, you claimed all ownership to the coke, letting the youngin off scott free."

DP was surprised at how much FP knew about him. "Ok, you know this, you know that, but please still feel free to let me know the purpose of you watching me."

FP took one more pull off the cigarette and passed the short to DP who to his surprise took it. "It's real simple, DP a lot of these niccas either don't know the game or don't respect the game. But you do, me and you are two motherfuckers who know the game and also respect that motherfucker. I just want to lace you with the game and knowledge I have for you to take back out there once you're released. You see me, I got life for putting trust into a motherfucker I called family and this bitch nicca had the nerves to throw me to the wolves. The only thing I asked in return brother is bless yo' boy with a phone line and a few pictures here and there. That's it, that's all."

This time when the lifer offered his new cellmate a Newport he took it. From that day forth they were inseparable. They were in their cell one day when DP asked FP what his initials stood for? "Say FP, what the fuck do FP stand for my nicca?" FP was on the bottom bunk so DP had to look down from the top bunk.

"My nicca, FP stands for Firing Pin. You see you can have all the guns in the world but without the firing pin them motherfuckers ain't worth shit. Now tell me what the fuck DP stands for."

DP jumped down from the top bunk, "DP stands for Double Portion, cause I had to have double in the streets," DP said as he clapped hands with 'Firing Pin.'

DP was brought out of his early memories of prison by the guard tower telling him rec was now over. DP stepped into his cell fresh out the shower. "What's good, FP?" FP was doing what he did best and that was law. He was the true definition of a jailhouse lawyer. The only thing

18

different between FP and other jailhouse lawyers was he didn't help nobody with their case, he only worked on his. Where other jailhouse lawyers will help anybody.

When DP walked into their cell FP took off his rimless gold reading glasses, "sup DP, I see you were out there dealing with that bitch shit." Dp rolled on some lady secret deodorant before turning around in the cell that was made for one person but the state of Wisconsin had two convicts sharing the space.

"FP my nicca, what the hell are you talking about, what bitch?" FP pulled out a box that had all rolled up cigarettes in it. He lit the rolled-up cigarette with some tissue and a spark from the wall outlet.

"DP my nicca, I'm talking about that bitch Mother Nature."

DP put on his all gray white beater before turning around to holler at his friend, "say fam, I was out there trying to get a grip on things. My nicca I get discharged Friday, that's four days away."

FP looked at him with a concerned stare on his face, "DP my man, that's a good thing isn't it?"

"Come on big homie, you know that's a great thing, discharging on a dime piece and that slut wasn't even fine."

"So, what's the problem my brother?" FP asked him while passing him the short on the rolled-up cigarette.

DP took two pulls off the tobacco filled paper cigarette before he dropped it in the silver stainless steel toilet. DP went to flush the toilet that sweated water at the bottom on a hot summer day when he noticed the roll up cigarette left a brownish residue on his thumb and pointer finger. He went to the sink that was connected to the sweating toilet to wash his hands. Even after scrubbing and leathering up with the Irish Spring soap it was still a light

19

brownish stain on his finger from ten years of smoking roll up cigarettes. "You know FP, I don't think I'll ever be able to get this fucking brown shit off my finger."

"Fam, you only been smoking them for ten years, try eighteen years and when you're gone I'm gonna continue to stain." FP held up the hand he smoked with. "These motherfuckers…" DP shared a condolence laugh with his friend of ten years, because he knew he was fighting a fight for his freedom.

"Dig FP, it really ain't no problem that I can't handle."

"So, lay it on me, my little brother."

"Thing is, the kid Butter who I took the case for and left in control of the things I built up from the ground is the man in the streets right now. And he's expecting me to step back in like I never left. But after doing this bid, I'm not ready to jump back out there head first into a new world of God, know that.

FP knew he had made the right choice by befriending DP. "DP listen my brother, you can get back out there and fall back into shit if you want to. If that's the case I'm gonna tell these nice pink people here to keep my cell empty cause yo black ass will be back."

DP went to speak when FP held up his hand. "Or DP, you can walk a fine line for about a year until I get out and we…." Fp stood up to face DP, "can go legit on some legit shit. My baby sister is doing her thing in the streets, she's all the help we need, the choice is yours my nicca."

DP looked FP in the eyes, "my nicca, what you mean now, you getting the fuck out? How, when nicca, you better not be fucking around with me," DP said as he gave FP a manly hug.

The two stayed hugged up for a few seconds before they parted. When they did part both men had smiles on their faces.

"Nicca, you can stop all that damn smiling and tell me when you found out this good ass news?" He asked as he went into FP's cigarette stash and grabbed a rolled-up cigarette. When he got a light off the wall outlet their cell lit up like the sky on the 4th of July.

"Well, homie, you know I stay on that law shit, and I had two top notch suits, private mouthpieces which cost a whole lot of money. That found loopholes in my case. That last good for nothing lawyer failed to look at or mention. It took 18 long years but the cop who arrested me was crooked as they came and got his ass kicked off the force. Somebody's phone recorded his snake ass planting a case on a young black boy who wasn't even a street kid. But like I was saying, just because you stay in the ghetto does't mean you're ghetto, ya dig."

DP inhaled the cigarette then passed it to FP. "So, big homie, why are you just telling me this shit, nicca?"

FP took a long drag of the cigarette before dropping it in the stainless-steel toilet. "My dude, I've been wanting to tell you and things, but I thought that shit with the guard a few years back was gonna catch up with me. And if it would've, then it would not have matter anyway. Somebody up there…" FP looked up to the top of the cell like he was looking into the heavens. "…Want to see me do the right thing, so they're giving yo' boy a second chance."

"Damn Fam, that's love, so what, your case is gonna be dismissed?"

"This is the thing DP, my mouthpiece told me that the judge is willing to hit me with time served. You know, to cover the state's ass from lawsuits and shit. So, it's gonna take a year to get me back into court just to get time served. I say about *10* months from now, yo' boy will be free G' once again."

The two sat around after that, playing chess, casino and dominos for the last few days before it was time for DP to get released. It was a nice fall sunny day for it to be the middle of October. The two convict's room in Waupun Max Prison was on the Northwest side of the building facing a rising sun. So, when the sun's bright and warm rays shined in their room on Friday morning, DP knew it was meant for him to go home. He laid on the top bunk just enjoying the warm sun when he felt FP knocking on his bunk from the bottom.

"Boom, Boom, Boom you up nephew?"

"Yeah, fam, I'm up."

"It's almost time, remember what we talked about. Get out there and lay lower than a snake until I touch down."

DP jumped down from his top bunk, hopefully, for the last time. He had packed all his belongings the night before and only had his state issued clothes, with the big brown heavy boots left in the cell. Alone with a state toothbrush which he used FP's Crest toothpaste to brush his teeth. After the two convicts did their usual hygiene routine, they shared one more rolled up paper cigarette before it was time for DP to leave.

"Dig, Big homie, it's that time. I put my baby sister's info in your box when you weren't looking. She doesn't know I'm getting out and I want it to stay that way. But look her up, she's a good person and needs a real man in her life." FP told him as they embraced for the last time in prison.

22

"I got you 'Firing Pin,' just make sure that you stay low in here till it's time to come home."

The guard was at their cell bars ready to take DP out. "Inmate #306278 let's go!" Once DP crossed the threshold of his cell he didn't turn around to look back. As he went ahead of the first shift transfer guard, you could hear DP's last words to his friend on the inside.

"One FP!"

Chapter 4

Arsenal had been running the T-Y-L crew since he was left in command by the former bosses. Ever since he's been running the crew, the T.Y.L click has been labeled the worsts organization in Milwaukee history. Arsenal had his hands and team into a little of everything. Murders, Robbery, Drugs, Extortion, Pimping and Pandering. Arsenal really didn't give a fuck about the former bosses and he felt that anybody in his click could be replaced if they had a problem on how he ran things.

Arsenal and two members out of the crew, Trigger and Baby Nine, were with him sitting in the parking lot of Auto Zone on North Ave. It was 11:30 pm at night so the car store was closed for the night. Baby Nine, the only female on the T-Y-L crew got out of the Mercedes Benz GLE to stretch her legs.

"Damn A, where the fuck is these Madison ass niccas?"

Trigger and the boss Arsenal got out of the Benz truck to stretch out with the voluptuous Baby Nine. Baby Nine was a redbone with long black silky hair that flowed down to the middle of her back. She was 5'7 and 135 lbs., the shape of her body kinda put you in the mind of the rapper Glorilla' fine ass.

"Shit! My mutherfucking ass is numb from sitting in this goddamn truck waiting on these out of town ass niccas. Shit!"

Trigger being the goofy one of the T-Y-L crew was always getting on Baby Nine's nerves. "Come on Baby

Nine, all that ass you got, the car cushion should go numb before that pretty mutherfucking ass."

"Fuck you Trigger, you just mad I won't sit on your face, perverted ass fool."

Trigger broke out in a big ass laugh and smiled. "Fuck it Baby Nine, just sit on my pillowcase and I'll be satisfied. You thick ass redbone you."

Before Baby Nine could say something back, Arsenal butted in, "Y'all kill that noise! Here come these mutherfuckers now."

Just at that moment a red BMW X6 pulled in the back of Auto Zone's parking lot where Arsenal was waiting. Once the fog lights on the BMW truck was turned off, the leader and his crew could see just how many people were in it. They only saw two guys occupying the two front seats of the X6.

"Ok you two shit talking motherfuckers, y'all move on my say so." The boss and his members moved in to shake hands with the driver of the X6 as both occupants got out of the wine-colored BMW truck.

"What's up A you ready to do this?" The driver asked him after their hands parted from their shake.

"Yeah, my nicca, let's make this shit happen before the fucking pigs come."

Arsenal and the driver from Madison stepped to the back of the BMW truck where the driver hit a button on the keyring and the trunk raised up. While Trigger and Baby Nine was in a stare down with a 300 lb. passenger of the X6. When the trunk came up, Arsenal could see two very large suitcases, he leaned over and unzipped the first one to reveal 50 handguns of every kind. 45's, 25's, 22's, 9's, 40's, 357's, 38's, 380's and Arsenal favorite handgun the

10-millimeters. The second suitcase contained 5 AK 47's and 4 Drake-O's.

"Aye Silencer, my nicca, I see you came through on these units here." The leader of the T-Y-L crew told the driver; whose name was Silencer.

"Come on A, you know this is what I do. Ain't shit changed from when I was supplying FP with toys, come on now," Silencer said with a 'Are you serious' tone in his voice. Arsenal was checking out the 10-millimeter.

"Well, Silencer, shit done changed now that I'm running the T.Y.L…"

Silencer looked Arsenal in the face. "Meaning what A?"

Arsenal cocked the 10-millimeter seeing that it was loaded. "Meaning, that was then, and this is now." The crew leader told Silencer as he pointed the loaded gun in his ex-street mate's face.

"Say A, what the fuck is you doing?"

"What the fuck it look like nicca? I'm taking these heats for me and my team."

"Fuck A, this shit ain't right. I was once a part of the T-Y-L and this how you gonna do me nicca? No, I'm not going," Silencer said as he launched towards Arsenal.

Silencer didn't stand a chance. Arsenal pulled the trigger on the 10-millimeter shooting him in the face and killing him way before he hit the ground. The passenger of the BMW turned his head towards the back of the truck when he heard the gunshot. Baby Nine and Trigger hearing gunshots took that as their que to jump into action.

Packing twin Glock 40's, the two released a barrage of 40 hollow point bullets into the fat man's body. Once the fat man's body slumped against the wine color candy painted truck, blood began to leak out the many holes in his own bleeding body. If you weren't up close you couldn't tell his blood from the truck's paint. Trigger rounded the truck to see the handguns in one of the suitcases because Arsenal had just finished zipping up the one with the assault rifle in it.

"Shit Arsenal, this is a lot of fucking burners," Trigger said as Arsenal handed him the closed suitcase.

"Take this to the whip and let's get the fuck out of here." He told Trigger while zipping up the other gun case. They were both ready to head back to their getaway ride when they both dropped to the ground clutching on their pistols.

"Baby Nine, what the fuck was that, you good?" Trigger yelled out from his and Arsenal's crouching position.

"I'm good pervert, fatboy looks like he can use one more hot one. Big boy still had life in him so I had to snatch it out. You and A can come on," Baby Nine said as she placed her 40 Glock back in its leather holster a couple inches away from her heated vagina strapped to the inside of her baby smooth thigh. Baby Nine pulled her high mini skirt down as she climbed into the driver seat of the X6 BMW. When she turned the key that was still left in the ignition the fog lights came on. That's when she saw Trigger and Arsenal dragging two huge black suitcases across the parking lot.

As they got closer she heard Arsenal say, "Baby Nine pop the trunk." After she heard the trunk close, that's when Trigger and Arsenal jumped in with Trigger in the front seat.

"Baby Nine let's get out of here before them people lock us the fuck up," Arsenal said from the back seat. Baby

Nine pulled out of the Auto Zone's parking lot and headed west to 77th and Thurston street.

Trigger was the first one to notice Clips, another member of the T-Y-L crew, in a midnight black RC sport Lexus Coupe. "Oh shit, I see the boy Clips is up in the trap. Come on BN park this bitch, so I can see if the boy got some of that loud, loud pack on him."

"Shut up Trigger and wait," Baby Nine said, as she parked behind Clip's Lexus Coupe and turned the BMW off. Arsenal was the first one to exit the truck.

"Since you two mutherfuckers are always talking shit, y'all grab that shit out the back. Shit talking mutherfuckers," Arsenal said, as he walked up to the house 7703.

Baby Nine pop the trunk of the X6 BMW with the keys as she shut the driver's door. "Trigger you better grab that shit because I'll be damned if I break one of my nails I just got done. What the fuck in those suitcases anyway that got my ass out here tonight fucking with you and Arsenal ass?" Baby Nine asked as she walked up to their trap house and went through the front door that Arsenal left open.

Even though Trigger and Baby Nine were always giving each other shit. They had nothing but love for each other, they were more like brother and sister.

Trigger said, "fuck you bitch," as he heard her Gucci heels click clacking on the sidewalk while he was left to grab the suitcases.

Once inside the house, Trigger closed the front door to see Baby Nine, Arsenal, Clips and Beam, the youngest out of the T-Y-L crew at the kitchen table smoking out the hookah.

"I know you fools saw me carrying these heavy ass suitcases, while y'all around the table getting y'all smoke on, out of my hookah machine," Trigger said, as he left the suitcases by the front door to take a turn on the hookah. As Trigger hit the hookah that was filled with bubblegum Kush, you could see and hear the thick smoke as it traveled through the Patron that was bubbling at the bottom of the gun shaped hookah that he paid $1,500 dollars to have it custom made to represent the T-Y-L crew.

Trigger tried to talk through the Kush smoke and almost coughed up the Wendy's he ate earlier. "Where is Shotgun fool ass? Damn, this shit is strong." Cough, Cough. Trigger asked as he spit into the kitchen trash can.

"Right here fool, I heard you and your weak ass lungs way the fuck upstairs," Shotgun the mastermind in the T-Y-L said, as he came down the spiral staircase.

Trigger spit one more time into the trash can. "What's up my brother, you bean pie eating mutherfucker you."

"It's just like a nicca like you to mock a culture of he says, she says so called beliefs. But since it's you, I got to look over the stupidity and stupid things that come out of the hole in your face," Shotgun said, as he went to the front door to grab the suitcases.

"Shotgun fuck you nicca. This hole in my face is good for your chick."

"Whatever Trigger, this is not gonna be a battle of wits, because clearly my brother I'd already won hands down," Shotgun said, as he emptied both suitcases of its guns.

Clips seen all the firepower hit the rundown carpet. Carpet that once upon a time ago was thick and heavy. And was like a kid inside a candy store as he ran out of the kitchen into the living room. "Now that's what the fuck I'm talking about. Heat on top of heat. I got dibs on that 2-2-3 and this here .40 with the extended clip hanging out the pussy on this fine bitch," the younger member out of T-Y-L crew said, as he started lining all the guns in order from smallest to biggest.

"Damn Clips baby, you're handling those toys like they're a pair of titties," Baby Nine said as she used her Gucci stiletto heels to walk in the living room to examine the guns she helped take from them out of town dudes.

Once Arsenal finished getting his high from the lines of powder cocaine he was doing off the kitchen glass table. He wiped his nose before standing up to join the rest of the T-Y-L crew in the living room. "Ok, you shit talking mutherfuckers listen up!" Arsenal told, his click of hoodlums. Everybody looked up from what they were doing to give their full attention to their leader. Arsenal stood at 6 '0 and weighed 240 lbs. who wore his hair in the Mohawk style and had all eyes on him. "The time has come for the T-Y-L to take this fucking city by storm, one dope boy at a time. We have guns. We have the killers. Now all we have to do is pick our prey and the rest is history," the boss said to his team

"Me, Trigger, and Baby Nine crazy ass just hit off this one kat for these guns," Arsenal said, using his foot to kick one of the 2-2-3's to demonstrate the words that were coming out his mouth. "So, what I need for you mutherfuckers to do, is hit up all the gambling spots, clubs, any and every hangout. Where the so-called ballers are at and show them bitches that Milwaukee belongs to the T-Y-L's now," Arsenal said picking up the 10-millimeter out of the pile of weapons and sticking it in the waistband of his

Roc pants. The rest of the members of the T-Y-L crew followed suit and started grabbing guns of their choice.

Trigger picked up an AK-47 in one hand and had a 2-2-3 in the other hand when he turned to ask his boss a question. "Aye boss, you know a lot of money making niccas hangout in club 'Rain' and club 'Us' chasing them bitches who go there to catch them a baller. So, what about Mz. Shelly? You know these joints are where Mz. Shelly conducts her business." Trigger asked the leader of the crew while checking himself out holding up the guns in the mirror.

Arsenal walked back into the kitchen to do another line of coke with the powder of cocaine around the rim of his nose. The leader turned around and faced Trigger, "My nicca, I wouldn't give a flying fuck who conducted business in any bar or fucking club. If any mutherfucker gets out of line, y'all have the tools to straighten their asses back out. I don't give a fuck who it is, and like I said, this fucking city belongs to the T-Y-L crew with a new H.N.I.C.," Arsenal said before burying his face back into the many lines of coke that was taking up half of the rectangle glass table that took up most of the small kitchen space.

Chapter 5

Mz. Shelly and her bodyguard Big Vest sat outside on the back patio at Shelly's mini mansion beach house that had its own private entrance to the lakefront. Sipping on Moet and Remy Martin enjoying the nice sunny morning. Big Vest took one sip of his drink and sat it down on the black stainless-steel patio table that sat between him and Shelly.

"Damn boss lady, I don't know how you're drinking this early in the morning," Big Vest said, lighting a Cuban cigar off the insect repellent candle that Shelly always kept lit anytime she sat on the back patio to think.

"Come on Big Vest, it's never too early to treat yourself while trying to get your mind right," Shelly said, as she took another sip of her Moet and Remy.

"Well, it's too early for me to get my drink on since I'm not really a drinker, but I will treat myself with this stogy here," the big man of a bodyguard said, as his dark full lips grip the inexpensive cigar as he inhaled the thick tobacco smoke.

"Vest, you know smoking that shit will kill you, at least fill up with some Kush instead of inhaling a mix of harmful shit that goes into tobacco."

"Come on boss lady you're talking to Mr. Hard to Kill himself. If these six holes in my chest couldn't stop me, what the hell is this good ass cigar gonna do to the Big Vest," he said standing up with his chest poked out and his hands on his hips like Superman.

"Boy sit down, yo' ass is crazy," Shelly said, as she let out a little laugh at the only person who had been there for her since her older brother went to prison some time ago. Shelly took another sip of her drink as she stared into the lake lost in her thoughts.

"Boss lady, what are you over there thinking about looking into that dirty ass water?" Vest asked.

"Just trying to get my thoughts in order, that's all Vest. You know I'm throwing that party for the boy Butter tomorrow and Boosie ass still hasn't hit me back yet."

"Chill out boss lady. Boosie Badass will come through. He hasn't let you down yet, so don't worry," Big Vest said, as he dumped ashes off his cigar over the patio rail on the many rocks that sat around, and under the Oakwood patio.

"I know Vest, I know. I also have been thinking about going up to the prison to visit my brother Silas. It's been a while, plus I've been missing him like crazy lately."

"So, do that then Shelly, what's stopping you?"

"Well, our cousin Marcus was supposed to call me back when he got time to go with me because he needs to talk to Silas too. Now, every time I try to call him his phone goes straight to voicemail," Shelly said as she sipped the last of her drink.

"Old Marcus huh, I haven't seen that boy in a while. What has he been up to lately?" Big Vest asked as he smashed his cigar out in the ashtray.

"You know the same ole shit. A little of this and a whole lot of that. Doing his thang from state to state."

"Is that right? Well, boss lady when you talk to him, let him know it's still love even though we went our separate ways," Big Vest said as he swatted at a fly that kept circling around his head. Big Vest smashed the fly

33

between his two big hands then wiped the remains on the leg of his pants.

"Ugh Vest, that's so fucking nasty," Shelly said with her face frowned up.

Vest just laughed at her. "Hahaha, so, boss lady, who's the kid Butter throwing the party anyway?" Big Vest asked as he checked his oversize hands for more fly guts.

"Yo ass need to go wash your hands. I swear you and my brother do some of the nastiest shit."

"I know why you think that, that's my A1-Day1 nicca."

"Anyway, Butter is throwing the party for the homecoming of his guy DP."

Big Vest said, "I saw DP a few times," before he remembered the face that went with the name. "Yeah, DP, I remember that dude. He started doing his thing a few years after your brother went to the joint. He was a money making nicca who didn't take no B.S in the streets. They say he went to prison because of the boy Butter. Word was, DP knew when one of his spots was about to get hit by those people. So, he told Butter who was a young kid then, not to keep any drugs in that trap house. Well, the boy was entertaining some hot tail girl in the living room, when the Feds and the Police kicked the front and back door in," Big Vest said as he picked up the remaining Cuban cigar and lit it once again on the insect repellent scented candle.

Shelly sat in her outdoor leather beach chair staring at him, waiting for him to continue the story. Big Vest took a pull off the hefty stogy before he went on with the story.

"Well, the police lined all three of them up on the living room floor. DP, the girl and Butter. Word was DP had a smile on his face because he knew there weren't any drugs there so he thought. Long story short, cops found 254

34

grams of crack cocaine and since DP was the oldest and who put Butter in the game at a young age, he claimed the drugs. And since it was his second dope case the judge laced his ass with *10* years in a *5* out, *15* years total."

"Damn that's some crazy shit, but the boy DP sounds like a stand-up type of nicca," Shell said as she fanned at the fly that kept flying near her face.

"If you need me to kill that one too, boss lady. Just let me know," Vest said holding up his king size hands.

"No thank you, but that's the story of DP huh?"

"Yep. Plus, DP left the boy Butter a kilo of dope even after he got him knocked for that long prison stay," Big Vest said, while taking a last pull off the stogy and tossing the butt on the rocks beneath the patio.

Shelly and Big Vest sat out there on the patio for about 45 more minutes. When Shelly's iPhone started ringing, she looked at the screen on her iPhone and saw it was Boosie calling her back.

"It's about time, Badass." Were Shelly's first words when she answered her phone while walking into the beach house with Big vest in tow behind her.

Chapter 6

As DP stepped out of prison a free man, he felt the weight on the inside being lifted off his shoulders. DP had to cover his eyes because for some reason the sun on the outside of prison shined much brighter, or so he thought. DP scanned the parking lot of Waupun's prison looking for his ride. The more he looked, he couldn't find any sign of Butter or his ride. Then out of nowhere DP saw one of the cleanest cars he saw in a long time. It was a Jaguar XF sitting on some 22-inch chrome factory Jaguar rims with tinted windows.

The XF stopped right in front of DP with its passenger side window coming down slowly. Once the window was completely down DP saw a smiling Butter sitting behind the driver's wheel.

Butter jumped out and gave his mentor a hug. "Damn DP, my nicca, a nicca has been missing you," Butter said, as he playfully punched DP in the arm. Who playfully punched back at Butter.

"Damn B, I see yo' ass done came up in the world." DP told his lil homie as he stepped back and gave the Jag a second look.

"Ah, you like this peace huh, big homie?"

"Yeah, Butter, I most definitely like this pretty bitch here," DP said as he walked around the Jag.

"I knew you would, that's why I brought this whip for you big homie. You just lost *10* years of yo life, fucking around with my mix up. After you told me not to keep the dope there, I did anyway trying to get some pussy from a freak chick." Butter told DP while staring at the pavement parking lot ground not wanting to look DP in the eyes.

DP who was dressed in a whole Gucci outfit, including shoes that Butter had sent him to get released in. DP stared at Butter, the young kid he came to prison for and left a lot of dope to, for about two minutes before he said anything. "So how do the clothes you sent me look?" DP asked, while dusting off his shoulders. Butter looked up from the ground to see DP standing there with the same smile on his face that he had *10* years ago before he came to prison.

"DP you look swole my nicca. I see you've been in there hitting them weights huh?"

"Yeah kid, ain't really shit else to do in the box, feel me?"

"Yeah, big homie I feel you."

"But dig this B, let's get the fuck out of here, I'm ready to put this shit hole in my rearview mirror," DP said as he grabbed for the door handle on the passenger side of the Jag.

Butter looked at DP getting in the passenger side of the car like he was crazy. "DP homie, what are you doing? I told you my nicca, I got this for you," Butter said as he walked around to the driver's side.

Once they both were in, DP turned towards Butter, "Say B, this one slick ass ride. Good looking on it, but I think it would be best if you drive back. You know, give me a chance to get used to riding in a car again," DP said as he found the button to let the passenger seat back.

Butter started the Jag that sounded like the wild cat growling in the jungle at night when it killed its prey. "I feel you my nicca, let's go get some more gear for the

37

homecoming of my nicca, D motherfucking P," Butter said happily, and glad to have DP back riding with him. He smashed out of the prison parking lot leaving a cloud of smoke as he did so.

The ride back to Milwaukee was shorter than DP's thoughts. Milwaukee had some new attractions added onto the city, but the city was still the same Milwaukee that DP remembered *10* years ago. Still ran down with drug infested neighborhoods, abandoned houses: three to 1 block. More liquor stores on more black corners. And the crime throughout the city was at an all-time high.

Once back in the city Butter took DP on a shopping spree that rounded off near *$15,000* dollars. The last stop was at Gino's jewelry store downtown Milwaukee where Butter already had DP a piece made. It was DP written in big cursive letters with white and baby blue diamond encrusted in the lettering; and the platinum chain that holds the DP medallion around one's neck.

"Here you go my nicca." Butter took the heavy necklace from Gino's son who took over the store after Gino retired from making jewelry, and placed it around DP's neck. DP checked himself out in the small mirror that sat above the glass showcase.

"Say Butter my young friend, you didn't have to get me this. You did enough with the ride and clothes."

"Say DP, this is the least I could do. Shit, you just done *10* fucking years, with no snitching and no bitching for my fuck up, feel me? Now let's bounce, so I can drop you off at the pad I got you so, you can get ready for your party." Butter told DP as they were buzzed out of the jewelry store.

Butter pulled up to a house on the 900 block of 90th and Good Hope to a single-family house. "Well, we're here old man." Butter told DP while turning off the Jaguar to help with his many bags and state property.

"So, Butter this is where you're camping out at?" DP asked, grabbing as many bags as he could out of the back seat and trunk.

"Something like that. I own this house but you will be the only one camping out here. I got a few properties around the city but I'm only camped out at one. That's my downtown condominium," Butter said as he unlocked the front door then passed DP the keys.

Once inside Butter left all the bags he grabbed at the front door and passed him the keys to the Jag also. "Here you go my nicca and make sure you are ready around *10* o'clock tonight."

DP caught the keys in the air as soon as Butter tossed them his way. "*10* tonight you say Butter?"

"Yeah, *10* my nicca, you need to meet with a few homies then it's off to the club. Boosie is performing and all. So be ready old man," Butter said as he turned to leave.

DP looked down at the keys in his hand and stopped Butte, "Say Butter, how you gonna leave if I got the keys?"

"Come on DP, I got this, I got my B.M.W 750 parked in the garage in the back. Only thing you worry about is being ready at *10* to get yo' party on," Butter said as he turned to leave, closing the door behind him.

Hearing the door close was like music to DP's ears. He left all his belongings at the front door to look around his new sleeping space. It was a two-bedroom house with both rooms upstairs. The living room had three-piece leather furniture set, straight from the Ashley store. On the walls were big framed pictures of Scarface, 2Pac, NWA and a naked picture of Pinky and Jade Fire, the porno stars. It was a square shaped glass table that sat between the

39

couch and loveseat. In the den to the left of the living room DP saw a King size pool table with a surround sound stereo system positioned nicely in the corner.

Upstairs in both rooms were king size beds with *50*-inch smart flat screen TV's mounted to the walls. Seeing the TV mounted on the wall got DP thinking. "This nicca doesn't have any TV's in the living room." He thought out loud as he made his way back downstairs to see if he missed a TV in the living room. DP walked into the living room and saw a metal ring hanging from the ceiling. He reached up and pulled on the ring and down came a *60*-inch projector screen. On the Ashley coffee table, there sat a black projector to match the Ashley furniture set. DP laughed at himself for missing the obvious. "One should've known." DP said to himself as he flopped down on the *$4,700*-dollar Ashley couch and grabbed the remote that was next to the projector, to catch up on *10* years of ESPN he had been missing.

He was about an hour into it when his eyes got heavy and he dozed off for a good rest.

Chapter 7

The gambling house on 13th and Hadley was known for keeping some of Milwaukee elite hustlers, and today wasn't no exception. When Clips and Baby Nine pulled up in Baby Nine's cream color two door Lexus coupe, they saw a line of whips of all makes, color and sizes.

"Baby Nine, you see what I'm seeing? It's got to be money in this bitch right now and I gots to have a piece of it!" Clips said, as he clocked his 45 Glock and stuffed it in the waistline of his basketball shorts.

Baby Nine pulled down the passenger side visor to use it to check her makeup. "Hold up Clips, let a bitch check her makeup before we roll up in this joint!"

"Bitch why the fuck you need to check yo' hoe-up, oops I mean makeup if we about to lay this motherfucker down. Huh, answer that?"

"For one Clips, watch your mouth before I unload my clip off into yo' young ass, for two, a bitch like me gots to look good in everything I do and three, you incest of a child don't make a move until I give you the heads up. Got that you special kid!" Baby Nine said, as she stepped out of the cream-colored Lexus coupe. Wearing a half AKoo top showing her belly ring and AKoo mini skirt that showed off her T.Y.L tattoo that went all the way up her leg to her vagina. With a pair of six-inch heels on.

Clips followed her out of her whip into the gambling spot. "Fuck you Baby Nine, with yo' fine ass." Clips said, as he slapped her on the ass as they walked inside.

Once inside Baby Nine whispered into Clips ear, "Remind me to slap the shit out of yo' young ass once we leave this shit hole."

Clips turned to her, "I love when you talk dirty to me," he said, as he made his way to the King size pool table where the dice game was taking place.

Sitting around the pool table, Clips saw three older dudes and two young ones. Out of the two younger ones Clips remembered seeing one of them whose name was 'Pyrex,' with the balling ass nicca Butter. So, he figured there had to be at least *60* bands in this gamble.

"Ok, the T-Y-L's are here so who got the dice next cause I'm gonna fade them."

The dice shooters around the table all looked at the young Clips like he was kidding, because he looked like he didn't have a pot to piss in or a window to throw that bitch out of. Wearing some Nike basketball shorts with some long Nike socks and a Nike wife beater with some Adidas sandals on his feet.

"Come on young fellow, this ain't no nickel and dime crap game. This is a grown-up folk's game, come back later, then younger guys of yo' speed will be out of school then, trying to lose their lunch money," the old man who was running the table said to Clips.

"Is that right?" Clips said, with a boyish grin on his babyface.

"Yeah youngin that's right, now take the little money of yours and go buy some Nike sandals to go with yo' school outfit. While we finish with grown men business. Now gone and get," the old man said, while shaking the dice in the dice cup.

The old man really didn't know who the T.Y.L members were but the two younger ones knew about the

T-Y-Ls and how they got down. So, they were just looking for the right opportunity to make their getaway. Clips knew he had them right where he wanted them.

"Ok old man with the big mouth, let's see if I can win me some Nike money. How about a game of 4,5,6 and I'll be the bank?"

The old man stopped shaking the dice in the dice cup to look up at Clips, "You say 4,5,6 huh, and you'll be the bank. How much does yo' bank consist of then young fellow?" The old man asked, letting his greed get the best of him.

"Well, let's see," Clips said, holding out his hand near Baby Nine.

Baby Nine who hasn't said a word since telling Clips she's gonna slap the shit out of him for smacking her ass went into her big sized AKoo purse and stuffed *10* bands in Clips small boyish hand.

"Ok my nicca, I'm in the bank. It's $10,000 in it right now. And I got another *10*…" Baby Nine went in her purse and pulled out another wad of money and held it up so that everybody at the gambling table could see it. "Bands to cover any bet here." Clips drop the *10* bands in the middle of the pool table.

"*10* don't cover. And since I'm the bank it's *$500* or better a bet, you motherfuckers ain't about to kill me and I'm taking pushes. So, if you motherfuckers are in, let's get it, if not go head and run back to y'all wives or baby mama's (BM)." The old men were all in because they figured they had young Clips.

Baby Nine finally spoke for the first time since threatening Clips. "Clips, gone and shoot the dice, all these ballers in here. I'm pretty sure everybody's in," Baby Nine said, looking right at Pyrex and the other young dope boy.

43

Not wanting to be done up by Clips, Pyrex and the other young baller both said, "Shoot the dice," while looking at Baby Nine. The dice game went on for about fort-five minutes and Clips got down to *$2,500* out of the *$10,000*.

"Man fuck this shit Baby Nine, give me another *10*. I'm raising this shit, it's now $1,000 a bet. So, you motherfuckers better come out of y'all pockets with some more cheese."

Everybody around the table went into their socks, pocket and boxer shorts and pulled out wads of cash because they felt at ease seeing young Clips lose *$7,500* fast. Then threw another *$10,000* in the pot.

"Ok motherfuckers let's get this money," Clips said as he rubbed his hands together like he was trying to keep them warm.

Baby Nine stepped in front of Clips, "Hold up Clips, let me get in this shit, because yo' young ass is losing all the fucking money with yo' young none dice catching ass." Everybody around the table laughed at Clips.

"Fuck you motherfuckers," Clips said as he let Baby Nine take his spot at the pool table.

It was Pyrex's turn on the dice, he put the two red dice and one green die into the small brownish kitchen cup and started to shake them. Pyrex had about *$6,000* bands in front of him for his bet, and another *$15,000* in a playmakers bag stuffed into his drawers.

Baby Nine felt it was time to bring the dice game to an end. "Fuck it, I got another *10* in my purse for some side money. Who wants some?" Baby Nine asked. As she went into the same purse the dice player's saw her bring out *20* bands an hour previous to this. This time everyone around the table waited to see her pull out another wad of cash but this time what they saw almost gave the old men a heart attack. Baby Nine came out of her Akoo purse with a small Glock .9 and aimed it at the men around the table.

At the same time Clips upped his .45 pistol and slapped the old man who was running the gamble. Who hit the dirty gambling house floor, that had ashes, cigarette butts, blunt roaches and spit from the many gamblers who gamble there. The old man was slow to get up and when he did, his forehead was busted open and leaking blood. The blood dripping on the old dirty green rundown that was covering the ragged pool table reminded Clips of himself when he was around five years old playing with paint at school.

The old timer covered his head with his hand to try and stop the bleeding while asking Clips, "Now youngin,' why you go and do that?" The old man said while wiping the blood on his already stained church shirt.

Clips pointed his pistol at the dice on the pool table and said, "Maybe because you slipped some loaded dice on me. You thought I didn't peep the move but old motherfucker I did. And to make sure you don't pull that shit on anybody else…" Clips pointed his gun right in the middle of the old man's face, "I'm just going to end this shit now for you." Clips pulled the trigger on his .45 pistol. The bullet entered the old man's eye socket leaving a hole that a pirate's patch couldn't cover up.

The old man fell head first into the corner pocket of the pool table. Clips turned towards his partner in crime. "Baby Nine, that's what I call a trick shot."

Baby Nine laughed at Clips young humor. "Boy yo' ass is silly. Now for the rest of you motherfuckers, if y'all want to get silly, be my guest and I bet I won't crap out.

45

Now throw all the cash, jewelry and phones next to the old man's head." Baby Nine told the remaining 4 gamblers.

Clips took Baby Nine's king size Akoo purse off her shoulder and started stuffing all the money off the table into it.

"Aye Baby Nine, I can see this ragged ass pool table through the back of his cheating ass head."

"Boy shut up and get the money so we can get the fuck out of here."

While Clips was busy filling her purse up with the cash, Baby Nine walked around the pool table right up on Pyrex's boxers while her right hand was gripped firmly around the handle and trigger of her .9 Glock pistol. "I'd take this my cute baller friend," she said as she pulled the Playmaker's bag from Pyrex's shorts.

Before she walked away she gave Pyrex a kiss on his cheek and told him, "I thought you were happy to see me but I guess it was just this money." As she walked away Pyrex couldn't help but to stare at the roundness of her plumped ass poking out of her Akoo mini skirt.

As Baby Nine and Clips made their getaway, Baby Nine looked over her shoulder and caught Pyrex staring at her ass and gave him a wink of the eye as they exit the front door. Before any of the four dice shooters could give chase, they all had to pull up their pants that Clips had pulled down, when he learned about Pyrex having a bag of money in his boxers. In doing this Clips came up on two pistols, a switchblade and another five bands out of the old man's slacks.

Once safely inside Baby Nine cream color Lexus, Clips pushed the start button and peeled off from the curb. Clips got about four blocks away when Baby Nine slapped him in the back of the head.

46

"Ouch, shit, what was that for BN?" Clips asked while turning up the music.

Baby Nine pulled down the sun visor once again to check her makeup. After applying some lip gloss, she turned to Clips and to give her reason, "That was for smacking me on my ass boy. Now head to the trap before I slap yo' ass again."

"Ok BN, I love it when you play rough."

"Boy shut up and drive," Baby Nine said laughing as she bobbed her head up and down to Rich Homie Quan old hit single.

Chapter 8

Butter had just left DP and met with Brick at club 'US.' An all nude strip club that was located on 3rd and North. Club 'US' building use to be a Walgreens, until Walgreens moved down the street and club 'US' moved in. So, it was the biggest in the state and attracted ballers from all walks of life and from all over. Even though the club was on the East side of Milwaukee, one of the city's dangerous neighborhoods, it still kept nice size crowds that most of the time went smoothly.

Despite the neighborhood, or the East side dudes who were known for drug dealing, killing and any other crime in the book, inside the club there were five stages. Four that were set in each corner of the club and the main stage that sat dead smack in the middle of the club. The bar itself had seven bartenders and took up the whole back wall of the bar. Hanging down over the bar were five, 80-inch flat screen TVs' that showed each stripper dancing at one of the five stages throughout the bar.

The club had an upstairs V.I.P. room, plus four smaller rooms in the back for those who wanted a private dance. The strip club also had a few booths and tables scattered throughout the place. Club 'US' was the place to be with a live DJ and all. So, it wasn't any surprise to Butter when he called Brick to get up with him and Brick said, meet him there. Club 'US' was one of Brick's favorite hangout spots, seeing that he done fucked almost every stripper there or was on his way too.

Butter walked into the club and scouted the area, looking for Brick. He knew to check all the booths or tables for him because Brick didn't do V.I.P. He liked to be right in the middle of everything and everybody. Butter spotted him at a back booth with two thick ass strippers keeping him company on each side of him. In the middle of the table at the booth, there was a bottle of Ace of Spade sitting in a bucket of ice, getting chilled. Also, on the table was a pack of New Ports, a bottle of Cîroc Vodka and *$700* dollars in ones and fives.

Butter pulled up a chair from a nearby table up to the booth and sat in it with the chair facing backwards.

"So, what's good Butter, everything went well with picking up yo' main man DP?" Brick asked him while pouring him a glass of Cîroc and taking the bottle of Ace of Spade off ice and chugging some. Butter took a swig of the Cîroc then took a cigarette out of Brick's pack and lit it with a book of club 'US' matches. They were sitting on top of the pack of New Ports.

Butter inhaled the tobacco smoke and blew it out through his nose. "Yeah, Brick shit was cool. I picked him up then we went shopping. I picked up his chain then dropped him off at the crib on Good Hope and told him to be ready around *10* tonight." Butter told Brick while taking another swig of drink and a pull off his cigarette.

Brick grabbed a handful of money that was sitting in front of him and stuffed it in one the strippers G-string who stood up on the booth seat and got to popping her big yellow ass right on the side of Brick's head. Butter looked at Brick like he had gone crazy.

"Nicca and you got the nerves to have yo' face frowned up. When I told you me and shorty were in a lip lock when I was a youngin. Nicca you can't hit any more

49

bottles, blunts or cigarettes of mine." Butter told Brick laughing at his most trusted soldier.

"Say Butter the human mouth they say is dirtier than a dog's mouth. And as you can see, this ain't the mouth," Brick said, while planting a kiss on both ass cheeks of the stripper.

Butter stood up and headed towards the abc for his private dance with Milk and Chocolate, the black and white strippers he had waiting on him. "If you need me, ass kisser, I'll be in the back fool."

Brick stops kissing the ass of the stripper long enough to say something to Butter before heading back. "Aye Butter."

"Yeah,"

"Since you're taking my white piece of meat send that pink bitch at the bar my way please," Brick said as he went back to kissing all over the now laughing stripper's ass.

Butter walked into the back private area to both strippers kissing each other with 'Love and Happiness' song by Al Green playing on the back-room system. Butter saw his bottle of Patron sitting on a small round coffee table and popped the cork. The two strippers walked over to him and gently pushed him down on the loveseat in the private room.

The black one named Night, bent down and whispered in Butter's ear, "Hey Butter, long time no see. You know this pussy has been missing you," she said as she took the white girl's hand and rubbed over her bare shaved pussy.

Butter took a nice size swallow of Patron. "Oh yeah, Night? Well, I hope you and this white girl are gonna show me how much," Butter said removing the white girl's hand off Night's shaved and pierced pussy and sticking it in her own mouth.

The white girl whose name was Pearl, was sucking on her own fingers like she was in a contest for money. Night gave Butter a kiss on his cheek while unbuttoning his pants and bringing out his stiff dick. "Don't worry about nothing daddy, me and my bitch Pearl got you. You just relax and enjoy these forbidden fruits baby." Night told Butter while pushing Pearl's head down to the tip of Butter's hard dick.

Butter, Night and Pearl was twisted up in a semi threesome on the loveseat when Brick busted into the room. "Sorry Butter, but we got to go. Ecstasy just hit my line and told me that Pyrex just got stripped at the gambling house on 11th street," Brick said, unable to take his eyes off Pearl's big round white ass.

Butter jumped up and pushed his manhood into his pants. "Brick, call Ecstasy back and tell her and Pyrex to meet us at my spot downtown cause I want to know what the fuck happened. I told his dumb ass about going to those types of joints by himself," Butter said pushing the two strippers out of his way. "Move Bitches!" Was all he said to Night and Pearl as him and Brick headed out of the back private room and club 'US' knocking Butter's bottle of Patron over in the process of doing so.

On the way out of the club Butter and Brick almost bumped into Trigger and Shotgun as they were entering club 'US'.

"Damn niccas, watch where the fuck y'all going." Trigger told Butter and Brick. Brick being the last out of the 2 turned around and told Trigger.

"Nicca who the fuck you talking to? I'll snap your neck playboy, if you ever come out of it sideways again towards us nicca."

Trigger, always looking to start some shit went to the pistol in the small of his back. "Nicca you must not know who the fuck I am. The name is Trigger cause I can't get enough of pulling them. From the T-Y-L crew so I'd be careful of what comes out of yo' shit hole my nicca."

Brick saw Trigger hand go to his pistol and was mad at himself for letting Trigger get there before upping his. Butter was behind Brick, so Trigger and Shotgun didn't see him take out his chrome Glock 40. "Say my niccas, either we can end this shit now..." Butter told them showing that he also was strapped. "Or we can really end this shit."

Trigger wanted to try Butter but Shotgun being the smart one out of them, knew it wasn't the right time. "Say Trigger my dude, let's get us some drinks and we'll deal out bullets at another wild west card game," Shotgun said defusing Trigger.

"Yeah, you're probably right Shotgun, plus I don't want my bitch Night to see any blood. Bitch gets a little light headed and shit. I ask the bitch what she does when she gets her period." Trigger told Shotgun as they walked away.

Brick heard Trigger say, "Another place, another time playboy," as they turned to leave. Still pissed about the whole situation, Brick yelled over the music coming out of the club, "Yeah, bitch niccas, another place, another time son."

Butter grabbed Brick by the back of his Roc shirt. "Chill Brick, it's too many witnesses and cameras around right now. Plus, we got to see what's up with the lil homie Pyrex."

52

Butter jumped into his 750 BMW and Brick cranked up his music in his Audi truck as the both of them pulled out of US's parking lot.

Chapter 9

Ecstasy, Pyrex, and Scale set around Butter's downtown condominium smoking Kush and drinking Remy. Scale, the super-hot head in Butter's money-making click, was staring out the window waiting for Brick and Butter to show up. Scale's name didn't come from weighing up a lot of dope; his name came from all the dead bodies that weighed up every time he pulled out his pistol.

Scale turned from the window to face Pyrex and Ecstasy, who were seated on the couch passing a blunt of loud between them. Scale was 5'11 and 180 lbs. with 360 waves. He took a drink right out of the Remy bottle.

Ecstasy, not the one to bite her tongue, got right on his ass. "Damn Scale, I'm glad that Butter keeps a stock bar here."

Scale raised his eyebrow and looked at her with confusion. "Meaning what E?"

"Meaning nicca, I'm glad because you got your pussy eater's all over the bottle," Ecstasy said almost choking off the weed from laughing at her own humor.

Scale took another swig of Remy right out of the bottle. "Really E, at a time like this you want to crack jokes and shit. Not right now Ecstasy, not right now. And for yo' young dumb ass, how the fuck you let some nicca and bitch catch you slipping, how? T-Y-L's, what the fuck is a T-Y-L? Niccas gone have to pay with their lives, y'all hear me? Yo' ass," Scale pointed a long boney finger at Pyrex.

"Luckily you didn't lose your life fucking around at that weak ass gambling death trap. Can't say the same shit about the old man, huh. And where the fuck is Butter and Brick? I'm ready to bust my gun," Scale said as he took another swig out the bottle and turned back towards the window.

Pyrex put the butt of the blunt in the ashtray and blew the smoke in his mouth out through his nose. "Say Scale, my nicca, I feel you and all. That's why I'm about to be a dummy. Yeah, I got caught slipping, but it's gonna be a whole different story when the shoe is on the other foot," Pyrex said placing his .380 gun on the coffee stand next to the sectional.

Just then the front door opened and in came Butter and Brick. Butter went to the fully stocked bar while Brick flopped down next to Ecstasy giving her a peck on her cheek.

"Stop Brick, don't be kissing on me, I don't know where your lips have been. Knowing you, yo' ass was probably at club 'US' tipping them nasty ass strippers," Ecstasy said, using her well-manicured hand to wipe Brick's kiss off her face.

Butter poured him a shot of Grey Goose and down the whole thing. "All I asked was for this day, the home coming of DP, my big homie to go smoothly. That's all I ask, that's all. Now yo' ass get stripped by who?" Butter asked Pyrex.

Before he could answer Scale jumped in, "His young ass got caught by a nicca and bitch that said they were with the T-Y-L's crew," Scale said, cocking his Tech-9.

Butter looked at Scale, "Ok Bumpy Johnson, calm down. Pyrex and Pyrex only. Tell me what happened?" Butter asked, while pouring himself another shot of Grey Goose.

Pyrex wiped the sweat that was brewing on his forehead with his hand. "It's simple B. I was over there on 11th street with the old man like I do every Friday. When this young cat and this bitch, popping off about the T-Y-L's crew, are in the building."

Hearing the T-Y-L's for the second time since they walked in had Brick's mind ticking. "Hold up a sec, P. Did you say the T-Y-L?" Brick turned towards Butter thinking the same thing.

"Hold up Brick, let Pyrex finish, go ahead."

"Yeah, I said, T-Y-L was what they were screaming. Anyway, the young boy had the bitch pull out about *20* bands like shit was good. Next thing I know the old man who runs the house is lying on the pool table dead and the bitch is pulling my money out of my boxers. As soon as I could, I hit Ecstasy and Scale on their line and they called y'all. So here we are now."

"How much?"

"Huh, Butter?"

"How much money did they get off you?"

"Oh, they got about *20* bands off me," Pyrex said, breaking down some sour diesel on the coffee stand.

"Ok, that was some light shit, nothing you would miss. This what I want done tomorrow, I want ears to the streets. I want all the information on these T-Y-L motherfuckers!"

Scale hearing the word tomorrow damn near busted a vein in his neck. "Tomorrow, tomorrow Butter, why tomorrow? We need to be out there now busting our pistols on these bitches," he said waving his gun around in the air.

"Listen Scale, tonight is the bash of the old head who taught me all I know, without him none of us will be where we're at now. So tonight, we celebrate. It's a fucking celebration. So, what I need for you motherfuckers to do…" Butter looked at the time on his Movado watch. "It's 8:30 pm, go get dressed so we can be at club 'Rain' by 10:00 pm. Let's make it do what it does."

Everybody started getting up to leave and do what Butter requested. "Pyrex, you know they are not gonna let yo' young ass in, so try not to get yo ass in anymore mix ups tonight, ok." Butter told him with his arm around Pyrex's shoulder as he walked him to the door. Butter gave daps to Scale and Ecstasy as they walked past him to leave.

Brick was the last one to leave when Butter stopped him. "Hold on a sec, Brick." When the others were on the elevator Butter closed the door.

"What's good God?" Brick asked him.

Butter looked Brick in his eyes. "Do you think those niccas were the ones to strip Pyrex. Because when we were having words, I could've sworn one of them screamed out the T-Y-L shit."

"You know what B, you're right son, I heard one of them kids speak that peace. But if what young Pyrex said is true. It wasn't any of those kids. Because he said it was a youngin and some shorty."

"Yeah, you're probably right Brick, but maybe they all run together. If so I want them bitches resume A.S.A.P." Butter told Brick as he gave him some dap to leave.

"You know I'm gonna do my homework on them nice people. Peace, one God," Brick said as he entered the elevator to head down to the underground parking lot.

Butter closed the door and headed to the shower to get ready for tonight.

Chapter 10

DP woke up to the sound of a ringing phone. He went through all his bangs until he came across a big face iPhone. He saw on the screen, it said Butter. But after being gone *10* years he didn't know how to work the phone. About six minutes had passed before he finally figured out how to connect the call.

"Hello?"

"DP."

"Yeah, Butter it's me."

"DP, don't tell me your ass was sleep."

"Hell, I was. I dozed off for a second watching the big ass thing of a TV," DP said, yarning trying to shake his drowsiness off.

"Well, DP I need for you to get yo' ass up and get ready, it's time to party and introduce you to my little circle."

"Ok, Butter I got you homie."

"Good, I'll be there in about an hour to get you my nicca." Butter told him before hanging up the phone.

DP set there on the couch for about two minutes trying to figure out was Butter still on the phone. And if he wasn't, was the damn phone hung up. DP said fuck the phone and laid it down on the couch and headed to the shower. It's been *10* years since he was able to take a shower by himself. So, DP enjoyed every minute of it.

Once out of the shower he found a closet with some large dry towels in them. After drying off, DP walked into the living room naked. He went through his bags and got some new socks, boxers and a wife beater out and put them on. He remembered seeing some cologne on one of the dressers, so he headed upstairs. In the master bedroom DP came across some Armani cologne and sprayed some on his neck, wrist and dick. Which in doing so, he had to fan down there cause the strong cologne was feeling like it was heating up. DP loved the smell of the Armani cologne. He could remember them long nights in prison reading GQ magazine and catching the sample pages with the smell goods and wiping them around his cell. Armani was always his favorite.

DP unzipped the bag to his tailor-made Giorgio Armani suit and took it off the hanger and laid it on the couch. DP chuckled to himself. "I was wondering why Butter kept on insisting I get the Giorgio Armani suit. I see the lil homie has great taste."

DP was dressed and looking like a million bucks, the last thing he had to do was put on his DP diamond necklaces. He picked up the big size jewelry box and opened it up to reveal his medallion. He took the heavy chain out and put it around his neck. DP went upstairs to check himself out in the wall mirrors he saw all around the master bedroom. Looking into the mirror, DP was loving what he was looking at. "OK, DP you're back out. Now the thing is staying out," he said to himself as he headed to the light switch on the wall by the door on his way out.

Before turning the light off and closing the room's door, DP took a look, really around the room. He saw a mirror line up all around the room plus, a big mirror on the ceiling over the bed. "Damn the boy is a freak," he said to himself while switching off the light and closing the door.

On his way back downstairs, DP heard Butter enter through the front door. "I see you found the Armani cologne on the dresser, huh?" Butter asked him smiling ear to ear.

"Yeah, Butter. I sprayed a little on. I felt it was only fit, seeing you got me this Giorgio Armani suit."

"Well, DP I ain't on no homo shit, but I must say that you are looking and smelling good."

DP descended from the top of the stairs and looked Butter over from head to toe. He was wearing a Gucci suit with Gucci loafers and the cologne he had on DP figured it was Gucci also. "Say Butter, I see you came a long way from the Urban wear style, huh kid?"

Butter laughed, "Yeah, DP you can say that, but I still get my Urban on from time to time." Butter told DP while opening the jacket to his suit.

As soon as Butter did this, DP was almost blinded by his chain. He had a stick of butter encrusted with yellow diamonds on the outside and in the middle, it said, 'Butter NoneFat in all black diamonds.

DP reached out and held Butter's chain. "NoneFat huh?" He said, letting the chain go and fall back unto Butter's chest.

Butter smiled at DP and said, "Yeah, NoneFat, meaning a chick can lick on me all day and not gain any weight." They both fell out laughing with tears almost coming out of their eyes. "Come on DP, let's ride. I want you to meet a few people," Butter said as the both walked to the front door.

Outside DP wasn't expecting to see a big white Excursion limousine. "Damn Butter, when you do it, you do it big don't you?" Butter looked at him.

"You told me you only live once."

They made it to the limo to have the driver open the suicide doors. Inside was Brick, Scale and Ecstasy all

60

dressed to impress. Where Butter and DP were seated, they were facing the other occupants in the limo. Butter past a glass fill of Ace of Spades champagne to DP.

"DP, I want you to meet Scale, Brick and the lovely Ecstasy. Everybody I want y'all to meet my nicca DP," Butter said pouring himself a glass of Ace of Spade.

Scale gave DP a head nod, Ecstasy gave him a sexy smile and a wink of the eye and Brick told him, "What's up God," with a fist bump. DP acknowledged them all back in some type of way.

They made it to the club 'Rain' about 11:15 pm and it was crowded. The driver pulled right up to the V.I.P. entrance and opened the back doors.

First, out come Scale, Brick, Ecstasy, Butter then DP. Once inside they were escorted to the V.I.P section of the club, all except Brick who said he will be there in a second.

Inside the club there were fine women everywhere DP looked. Inside the V.I.P room the shit only got better. It was all DP could drink there but he was taking it easy for now. They were in the club for about an hour when Badass got on stage and did his thang. Boosie performed some of his greatest hits that got the club jumping harder than the V.I.P room with his presence. Which had all the groupies flocking his way. Boosie even stopped by their table before he left and said what's up to Butter.

Out of all the females in the club who were trying to get DP's attention, DP only had eyes for one. She was wearing an all-white see through Louis Vuitton one piece bodysuit. DP didn't know who she was, he only saw her speaking with the V.I.P. DJ and bartenders a few at a time then disappearing back out the club.

Butter got up and excused himself. "Alright people, I'll be right back, gots to drain the snake," he said walking off. Butter got about two feet away when Brick came out of nowhere and followed him to the washroom. Brick didn't let Butter go too far by himself in a place like this because he didn't trust many and after that shit took place earlier, he was on extra guard.

"Her name is Mz. Shelly, and she own this club and the strip club on the East side called US."

DP looked at Ecstasy with a busted smile on his face. "Pardon me, ummm Ecstasy is it?"

"Yeah, Ecstasy and old girl you've been having yo' eyes on with the see through white on. Her name is Mz. Shelly," Ecstasy said offering DP a Newport. "Do you need one?"

DP took the cigarette after lighting it up and taking a pull, he looked at Ecstasy really good for the first time. She was wearing a 2-piece Gucci outfit with the heels to match. Her hair was in a weaved Bob style that gave a person clear viewing of her smooth face. "How do you know I was looking at her Ecstasy?"

"DP don't let this sexy face and banging body fool you. It's a reason why Butter got me employed and it's not because of these things." Ecstasy told him while taking a drink of her Long Island iced tea.

"Well, I got you Ecstasy, but I have been gone a longtime and she was sure of something to look at."

"Well, shit, what the fuck am I?" Ecstasy asked giggling.

"Not saying it like that. You're a looker yourself ma, but word is you're family. Plus, I already saw who you got eyes for."

Ecstasy almost spit out her drink. "What? Who do I have eyes for, DP?" Ecstasy wanted to know, enjoying the conversation her and him were having.

"Well, even though I have been gone a while I still know the signs and the way you look at…" Right then Butter and Brick came back from the washroom.

"So big homie is you enjoying yo'self?" Butter asked over the music.

"Yeah, Butter this was love homie." DP told him while jumping up to give him a hug.

"That's what's up my nicca. Come let me introduce you to some of these bitches I know up in here." Butter told him.

DP sat the drink down that was in his hand on the table facing Ecstasy. DP looked her right in the face. "Ok, baby girl, I'm gonna go with this fool so I'll holler at you later."

"That's what's up DP. Welcome home," Ecstasy said holding up her Long Island iced tea.

DP turned around and told her. "Good looking ma. Now have fun with your boyfriend." DP turned around and gave Brick some dap. "Good looking on watching Butter's back."

"No doubt. You know that's my man." Brick told him in return.

DP turned around and gave Ecstasy a wink of his eye. Ecstasy knew he was talking about Brick now and she fell out laughing.

Brick looked at her like she was crazy. "What's funny Ma?"

Ecstasy just looked at him and rolled her eyes. Not trying to pay no attention to him.

When DP caught up with Butter, he was at a table talking to a group of females that was barely wearing anything. "Ladies, this here is my big brother from another mother. He just came home from doing *10* years in the pen. So which one of y'all gonna give him some pussy?" All the females at the table fell out laughing at Butter. But really all of them wanted to be the one to give DP some pussy.

Chapter 11

Mz. Shelly had just given Boosie a cut of the money from the door before he was off to do a show somewhere else. She was headed to her back office when she saw some drunk niccas being overly aggressive with a female who looked like she had too much to drink. Shelly looked around the club to try and find Big Vest or any of her security team.

Club Rain was known for having a big turn out and with Boosie performing that night, the club was really overcrowded and she couldn't see any of them. The club only had one blind spot and these low lives have found it. Shelly didn't want a lawsuit or the cops running around her place so she had to think of something fast. Someone had left an MGD bottle on a nearby table. Shelly bent down and cracked the bottle on the floor of the club. To somebody looking her way, it looked like she was bending down to wipe her shoes off.

As she approached, Shelly could see three dudes. Two of them were heavyset and the other one was a short thin guy, the two heavyset dudes was holding down a thin white girl, while the thin shirt guy was trying to position himself between her legs. Shelly entered the blind spot like she had too much to drink and was looking for the washroom.

"Uhm excuse me, but a bitch has to piss. While y'all all in the way trying to get y'all freak on with some thot white bitch. See that's the problem with niccas, y'all always leaving the sista to go be with Becky with the good

65

hair," Shelly said pretending to bend over and clutch her stomach like she was gone be sick. "Damn, I think a bitch had too much to drink. Where is the washroom, shit?" Shelly asked holding up the wall ready to strike out with the broken beer bottle.

The three rapists turned around to see what they thought was a drunk Shelly leaning on the wall. "Aye y'all see what I see, my nicca. This place is just crawling with bitches trying to give up the pussy," the shortest one said standing up. He walked up to Shelly, "Yeah, come on, the shitter is this way, I'll show you where it is bitch."

He tried to push Shelly against a corner wall but she sidestepped him and jabbed the broken beer bottle right into his neck sending him screaming to the floor while leaving a work of blood art on the wall. The two big guys saw what happened to their comrade and let the white girl go to confront Shelly. The white girl jumped up happy to be free and bolted right past Shelly, didn't even try to pull her with her.

Shelly mumbled under her breath, "Damn, bitch I was here to help you and you just gonna leave a bitch stuck?" When Shelly turned around, the two big lowlifes were right in front of her. Shelly looked down at her hand and saw that most of her beer bottle broke off in the short one's neck, who was on the ground screaming.

"Fam, get that hoe, the bitch stabbed me," he said trying to use his hands to stop the bleeding.

Shelly had to think of something fast because she was in trouble. The biggest one grabbed Shelly by the neck and lifted her up on the wall by it.

"Bitch, you about to pay for stabbing my little brother." Shelly was losing her breath fast.

DP looked up to see Butter making out with two females in the corner of the V.I.P room. Brick and Ecstasy was still at their table deep in conversation and Scales was at the DJ's booth talking with the DJ. DP decided to check out the rest of the club and slipped out of the V.I.P room undetected. DP was on his way down the stairs when he spotted Mz. Shelly going off in a dark corner of the club. Still strongly attracted to her, he followed her to see if he could get her to have a conversation or even buy her a drink.

DP had to smile at the thought of buying the owner of the club a drink. DP was almost on her when he was stopped by some thirsty looking female.

"Damn, honey don't I know you and if I don't I'm trying to get to know yo' fine ass." She told DP rubbing on his DP necklaces.

DP took the necklaces and put them away in his shirt. "How are you doing, Ma? Look, I'm kinda in a rush so maybe I'll get a chance to talk with you later," DP said trying to step around the woman who was obviously drunk.

"Not so fast, mister tall and sexy. How about me and you mosey on to the bar and you buy me a drink, handsome."

DP was getting tired of playing with the intoxicated woman. "Look you fat oversize lady. Why don't you mosey yo' sweaty ass over to the bar and buy some gum, because yo' shit ain't right!" he said stepping all the way around her. DP got to the spot where he thought he saw Shelly dip down and swear he heard a cry for help.

*   *   *

Shelly knew that she better do something fast because the room was getting dark by the minute. She took her two thumbnails and tried to dig out the heavy guy's eyeballs. The big man let out a yep when he felt her nails go inside his eye socket and dropped Shelly back to her feet. As soon as Shelly's feet hit the ground her heel gave away and she twisted her ankle. Sending her to the ground. Soon as she tried to get up, the last rapist kicked Shelly square in the chest, sending her flying deeper into the blind spot. Shelly tried to stand and found she couldn't, due to the fact her ankle might be broken and her breath was coming up short because she just got kicked in the chest by a size fourteen.

The fourteen sized shoe weaning man towered over Shelly. "Bitch, you done fucked up. I guess you can pay with some of that pussy."

Shelly on her hands and knees tried to scoot away from him.

*   *   *

DP got four feet into the blind spot and couldn't believe what he walked in on. On the ground was a short man that looked like he was losing blood out of his neck.

Then he saw two big guys towering over Shelly and one had streaks of blood running down his face. DP had just done *10* years in prison and most of that time he was working out so he wasn't worried about the two bigger guys. DP was bench pressing 380 lbs. and he was great with his hands.

"Damn, all this free pussy out there and you three clowns are trying to take something. I mean y'all are some ugly niccas but I'm sure it's a bitch out there for y'all."

As soon as the one with the blood streaks on his face turned, DP hit him square in the throat crushing his windpipe and sending the man right to the ground, knocked out. The short guy said something and DP turned and kicked him right in the head. Smashing his skull on the wall leaving a blood stain like a person bouncing a basketball in some red paint and threw it against the wall.

When DP turned around he was rushed by the last remaining big guy who pushed him into the wall sending DP phone sliding into the corner. DP recovered and gave the big man three quick punches to the ribs, pushing him back a few feet. The man tried to rush DP once again and found out he was no match for the shape DP was in. DP hit the man so hard in the right ear that he lost the sound in both ears for a second. The disorderly man swung a hard right that caught DP on the side of his neck, that staggered him back a foot.

DP was tired of playing with the overweight man and in his mind, he set out to finish him. When out of nowhere Big Vest and three members of the security team and the still crying white girl came and grabbed DP and the last standing rapist.

*   *   *

Shelly watched as the man came to her rescue. The guy was clearly in good shape, as he went to work on her attacker but who was he? Shelly couldn't help herself from staring at the man muscles as they were seen through his tailor-made suit. Shelly heard the sound of Big Vest and a few of her security team. She looked up to see them take a hold of DP and the three rapists. Big Vest saw Shelly on the floor in the corner of the blind spot and rushed to her side.

"Boss lady, are you ok?"

"Yeah, Vest I'm ok. I twisted my ankle trying to stop these nasty ass rapists' motherfuckers' from raping that white girl." Shelly told him as he helped her off the floor.

"I'm glad she came running past me and fell or I probably wouldn't have known shit that was going on. So, Boss lady, what you want me to do with these four motherfuckers?"

Shelly put most of her body weight on Vest, she used her arm that wasn't around Big Vest's neck to point at the men. "Those three motherfuckers take in the back and beat the living shit out of them. Make sure these bitches don't ever want to step foot back in any club. And him…" Shelly pointed a broken finger nail in DP's direction. "Make sure that anytime he's in here his drinks are free." Shelly told Big Vest as he helped her into her office.

One her way there she passed DP and said, "Nice hands," and gave him a smile that had DP wanting to know any and everything about her.

Chapter 12

When DP made it back into the lights of the club, he wondered how long he'd been back there because the crowd was dying down, he was about to head back to the V.I.P area when he spotted Butter and the rest of the circle approaching him.

"DP we've been looking for you big homie." Butter told him with his arm around two thick ass females who looked like they were holding Butter up from having too many drinks.

Ecstasy with her arm around Brick's lower back said, "I bet I know where the old head has been," laughing.

DP looked at her and gave her a playful mean mug, like mind yo' own business and then he let out a small laugh. "Nawl, it wasn't like nothing like that, but I will say it was worth the experience though," DP said as they walked out of the club and into the waiting limo.

With two new females added to the circle. Their next stop was getting something to eat at Michael's restaurant located on 24th and Wisconsin. Everybody was having a good time, even DP. Everybody got dropped off to their designated spots, with only DP, Butter and the two females who were with Butter being the last ones left.

The driver pulled up at the house where DP will be staying. When the driver opened the back door, DP stepped out with Butter right behind him.

"Aye DP, hold up a sec," Butter said.

"What's good B?" DP asked, starting to feel the little alcohol he was sipping all night.

"Shit big homie. I just want to say it's good to have you back. Whatever I got, it's yours, my nicca," Butter said slurring his words as he gave DP a manly hug.

After their embrace DP told Butter, "Listen Butter, my nicca. I want to tell you that I'm proud of you for how you're handling yo' business. Your people seem like some real loyal type of kats, that's love. The things you hit me with and the party and all this shit." DP waved his hand at the house and Jaguar XF in the driveway to indicate what he was speaking about. "It's all love my nicca, but I know that you're waiting for me to jump back down and be that nicca again like I never left. All that's understanding and shit but all I ask is for you to give yo' boy a little time," DP said while giving Butter some dap.

"Ok DP, I feel you big homie, take all the time you need, what I got my nicca nt going nowhere, but for now I'm about to see what shorty'em on," Butter said nodding his head towards the limo.

The two shared a little laugh as Butter headed back towards the limo and DP walked to the front door of the house. DP had just put the key Butter gave him in the lock and unlocked the door.

Butter stood up in the Excursion limo shouting out the sunroof, "Aye DP, welcome home my nicca, and this one said she is staying with you tonight."

At that moment the limo door opened and out came the light skinned female out of the two. DP took one look at her and knew he wasn't telling her no.

Once inside the house, she got right up on DP, "I hope you don't mind but I would like to take a shower first."

DP pointed upstairs, "Second door on the right, and it's towels in the closet next to it."

Her name was Flower, and her body would blind a person with 20/20 vision. When she got to the top of the stairs, Flower shredded her Missme tight jeans and shirt to reveal her birthday suit as she took the stairs one at a time. DP haven't seen a female naked in years and he had to admit that Flower body was something to write and tell FP about.

Thinking about FP, DP looked by the door to see his prison property still there unpacked and made a mental note in his head to go through his things to get FP's sister number to call her because he had a few dollars he wanted her to send FP for him. DP made it upstairs and heard the shower running in the bathroom as he made it into the master bedroom. In there he saw a green lighter on top of the dresser sitting next to the bottle of Armani cologne and used it to light a few candles Butter had around the room. DP turned down the bed to unveil some silk and satin sheets when he heard Flower behind him.

"Ooh, is that silk and satin sheets, they just do something to my body. It makes me want to stay in bed and have sex all day." She told DP as he turned around to see her drop the large dry towel from her curved body.

DP dick instantly started to rise to attention. Flower walked up to DP and he could smell the dove soap she used in the bathroom on her body. Flower starts whispering in his ear. "From the moment I saw you tonight I knew I had to have a piece of you." She told him as she took off the last piece of his clothing.

She aggressively pushed DP down on the king-sized bed and started to lick him from his neck, stopping at his nipples to give them some attention, then using her tongue to make a beeline to his rock hard dick. Flower used her tongue to lick up and down his dick until she got to the tip of his dick head where she spit on it.

Then used her hand to cover his whole dick with it. After doing *10* years in prison DP had enough of jerking his own dick. So, he would be damned if he let her do it. "No hands ma, I want all mouth."

Flower looked up with DP dick in her mouth and mumbled out the words, "Yes daddy." Flower was doing her thing giving him head that DP knew the pussy had to be the shit. With his dick still in her mouth DP checked the nightstand next to the bed looking for some condoms. He pulled out the bottom drawer on the nightstand to find two boxes of Magnum rubbers. DP opened one of the boxes and ripped one off the three pack.

DP gently grabbed Flower by her hair off his wet slobbed up dick and roughly pushed her down on the bed on her stomach. DP stuck his hand between her ass cheeks to rub her soaking wet vagina as he used his mouth to rip open the condom pack. DP could feel the heat coming from Flower's pussy as she begged for him to fuck her.

"Come on daddy, fuck me, please fuck me."

DP unrolled the rubber onto his dick and mounted her doggy style. Her pussy was so wet and tight DP almost blew a wad after a few strokes.

After fucking her doggy style for a few moments, Flower pulled his dick out of her pussy. "Before you bust that nut, I want to ride that dick," she said pushing DP on his back and inserting his dick in her as she rode his dick backwards. Flower was enjoying seeing herself in the mirror being a cowgirl, so she really got to bouncing on DP's dick. Dp was really enjoying his first piece of pussy in *10* years.

When he looked up to see Flower nicely round ass making his dick disappear every time she went down and reappeared every time she came up. The sight became too much for him as his toes started to cross and he released his first nut and slid in some pussy in *10* years.

"Damn ma, you got some nice shit between yo legs," Dp said as he was trying to catch his breath while pulling off the now used rubber and dropping it in the small trash can next to the nightstand by the bed.

Flower got up to use the bathroom and told DP, "I was thinking the same about you, that's why I ain't done with you."

DP just smiled as he lit up a Newport. DP and Flower sexed each other for the next two days, way into the late hours on Sunday night through Monday morning.

Chapter 13

Butter pulled up to Mr. Kirkland's private law firm to do business with his plug, Mr. Kirkland himself. He popped the trunk so him and Brick could grab the Gucci bags that contained the *$500,000* dollars. *$250,000* was for kilos of coke that Butter got every six months from Kirkland, and the other *$250,000* Butter gave to him so that Kirkland could set up in a business account overseas that the feds couldn't touch.

Butter and Brick got off on the 6th floor and entered the doors to Kirkland law firm's office where they were greeted by Linda, Kirkland's receptionist.

"Good morning."

"What up Linda, can you tell him we're out here to see him?" Butter told her back.

"Yes, I can, right away sir," Linda said to Butter while picking up the desk phone and staring at Brick. Butter noticed every time they were there Brick and Linda always flirted with each other. "Good morning Mr. Kirkland, yes they're here. Ok I'm sending them in now," Linda said as she replaced the phone back on its receiver. "Ok guy's Mr. Kirkland is ready for y'all now."

Butter and Brick walked pass Linda's desk right through the double doors that led to Mr. Kirkland's office. The office was a nice one. On the walls were heads of a lion, moose, bear and a rhino that Kirkland killed himself on his many hunting trips all over the world. His desk was made out of red oak and it was big enough to serve Thanksgiving dinner on it. He had a reddish leather couch sitting off in the corner and two reddish king size recliners sitting right in front of his desk. And a pearl white one that Kirkland set in himself. He had a large size fish tank that was home to some baby sharps.

There were some all black drapes hanging over the windows so you couldn't look out or nobody could look in. Plus, the carpet was so thick that as soon as you stepped a foot into it, it disappeared. Butter and Brick dropped the three Gucci bags right on top of Kirkland's desk.

"$500,000, $250,000 to go into the account and *$250,000* for the best shit money can buy," Butter said as he and his trusted soldier Brick flopping down in the expensive recliners.

"Hello to you also Butter," Kirkland said while pushing a button to reveal a hidden walk-in safe."

Kirkland took the money and stored it in the wall safe. It was a button on the inside that he pushed to close the safe as he set back into his chair. Kirkland offered them a Cuban cigar while lighting one himself. Butter and Brick both declined as they watched the smoke from Kirkland's cigar float towards the ceiling.

"So, Butter where's DP?" Kirkland asked as he put his *$5,000*-dollar Ralph Lauren loafers on top of his red oak desk.

Butter looked at him with a big smile on his face. "Shit, far as I know, his ass is still laid up with Flower."

"Flower, who is this Flower you speak of?" Kirkland asked with one of his eyebrows up.

Butter and Brick both gave a little laugh when Brick said, "A piece of pussy that I didn't have the pleasure of tapping yet son. So, if you have any ideas, God you're gonna have to wait in line B cause I'm on that next time she comes my way," Brick said trying to give Butter who moved his hands out the way for some daps. "Aye son what's that about B?"

Butter was laughing at him. "Come on Brick, you know Ecstasy will bust that head if she catches you sniffing anywhere around Flower pussy or any pussy for that matter."

"Oh, that's how you feel huh, God?"

"Naw Brick, that's how she feels."

Butter and Brick were both laughing when Kirkland said, "Aye Brick, if you need a lawyer don't call me that Ecstasy is something else." All three of them fell out laughing. "Listen Butter, your shipment will be at the normal pick up spot in two days. And when was the last time you saw DP?"

Butter said, "Friday late night."

When Brick said, "More like Saturday morning," as the two stood up to leave.

"Well, today is Sunday Butter, make sure you get in contact with him. And let him know I will have that ready for him on Monday afternoon," Kirkland said walking them to the door.

The three shook hands when Butter told Kirkland "Cool, cool. I have been calling his phone but he hasn't been answering. So, I'll ride by the house later." Butter and Brick headed to the elevator.

Chapter 14

Arsenal pulled into the parking lot of the club Rain. He had heard what had happened to Shelly and had to see it for himself. It was only noon but Arsenal knew that if Shelly was there this would be the perfect time to catch her. He looked around the lot but the only vehicle that looked familiar to him was Big Vest black hummer. Arsenal walked in and was greeted at the door by Big Vest.

"What's up Arsenal, what brings you down here?" Vest asked him as they exchanged fist bumps.

"Damn Big V, I need a reason now to come and talk with you and her?" Arsenal pointed towards the back where he knew Shelly's offices were. "We once were all T-Y-L's. Now I have to make an appointment just to rap with my people." Arsenal told Big Vest with his hand over his heart like Big Vest had hurt his feelings.

"Naw Arsenal, nothing like that playboy. All I was saying is that it's been a while, that's it my nicca." Big Vest walked Arsenal to the bar as he walked behind it himself and grabbed two glasses, and a bottle of Hennessy. He pours him and Arsenal a drink.

"Since it's been a while, have a drink with me before I let the boss lady know that you're here."

Arsenal had downed the drink when he looked at Big Vest and said, "You call her boss lady now, Vest?"

Big Vest drank his drink then slammed the glass down on the counter. "Let me go get boss lady." Big Vest stopped in his tracks and told Arsenal over his shoulder.

"Let's not forget Arsenal, she was your boss once upon a time ago, and for the record, she's the reason you got the juice now because she stepped down. So yeah, I'll let the boss lady know that you're here," he said walking towards the back where Shelly's office was located.

Shelly told Big Vest to send Arsenal in and don't worry about patting him down. Big Vest escorted Arsenal to the door that led to Shelly's office.

"Boss lady in there, and remember Arsenal, even though I'm out of the game, I'm still Big Vest so please be respectful or the crew that me and my boy FP started, I'll tear that motherfucker down. Go ahead, she's waiting."

Before Arsenal opened the door, he looked Vest in the eyes. "I hear you and shit Big Vest, but remember y'all left" Arsenal used his hand to point at the door where Shelly was on the other side waiting. "And I stayed and continued to rep T-Y-L so that shit you're popping off about…" Arsenal gave a little laugh, "You can save that shit my nicca. And oh, for the record she's your boss and to me… just another piece of fine ass I never got the chance to fuck," Arsenal said as he turned the knob to walk inside Shelly's office.

Big Vest closed the door behind him, Arsenal heard him say, "Be careful Arsenal, be careful."

* * *

Shelly was at her desk crunching numbers on her laptop doing paperwork. Resting her sprung ankle on a foot cushion when Arsenal walked in. Shelly removed her Burberry reading glasses and set them on top of the many stacks of papers on her desk. Arsenal took a seat on the couch in Shelly's office because he knew Shelly B.K.A. Mz. Shells was always ready for whatever was headed her way. When Arsenal took a seat on the couch and propped his leg up, Shelly had a laugh.

"So, what Arsenal you don't trust me?"

Arsenal looked at Shelly like she was crazy. "Hell, Mz. Shells opps, I mean Shelly. You always taught me not to trust anybody, so to answer your question. Hell no, I don't trust you or that big ass guard dog Vest you got as far as I can throw y'all; and you see how big Vest is."

"Well, I know this ain't no T-Y-L reunion because last thing I remember you said, once we leave wasn't no coming back. So, what do you want, Arsenal?"

"Well, Mz. Shelly I'm here to offer you a proposition on something that I got brewing."

"You say a proposition. A proposition on what Arsenal?" Shelly asked him as she repositioned her ankle on the foot stool.

"For one Shelly, I'm offering you the chance of never having that," Arsenal pointed at her foot, "Happen to you again. Look, me and my T-Y-L's are about to have this city on lock. All I need from you is to have both of your clubs for my headquarters and to scout out our baller victims. So, what do you say?" Arsenal asked Shelly while standing up off the couch.

Shelly started to laugh when she heard Arsenal's proposal.

"What's so fucking funny Shells?" Arsenal asked while tapping on the fish tank that was positioned inside the wall.

"What's funny is you Arsenal. You bring yo' ass in my shit like I owe you something, nicca I don't owe you or the T-Y-L's shit. Get that through your fucking mind and stop tapping on my fucking tank," Shelly said getting highly aggravated.

Arsenal stopped tapping on the tank and turned around to face Shelly. "You know Shells? I thought you were gonna be smart about this situation but I see you're being dumb like others."

"Others like who Arsenal?" Shelly asked with her hand caressing the *12*-gauge that was strapped under her desk.

"Never mind that, just mark my words Shells. Whoever ain't with the T-Y-L's, they're against us, meaning it's fair game on ex-members and the money making niccas in the streets." Arsenal told her with a deep threatening tone in his voice.

"Arsenal, let's get something understood. If you ever come in my place of business talking out the side of your neck again I'll put this legit shit to the side and come out of retirement to destroy everything you love. You wanna be me and my brother, but honestly, you don't have the balls to do what we did. Now get the fuck out of my shit before I have Big Vest drag you out."

Arsenal, having his ego crushed, started to walk towards Shelly's desk. "Bitch, fuck you and your brother. If you ever talk to me in that manner again I'll…" Arsenal got to the front of Shelly's desk where he was greeted face to face with Shelly's *12*-gauge.

"You'll do what Arsenal?" Shelly asked as she cocked the *12*-gauge that was an inch away from Arsenal's nose. "I can't hear you motherfucker!"

Arsenal tried to look at the tip of the gauge and his eyes crossed because it was too close to his face. Arsenal started to back paddle towards the door. When he felt the door knob at his back he starred Shelly in the face. "I see you got more balls than your faggot ass cousin but just like him, you done sealed your faith bitch. Remember I came to you first with a friendly offer, next time we cross paths shit won't be so friendly," Arsenal said as he twisted the knob to leave.

As he opened the door he ran right into Big Vest's chin. Arsenal had to look up to look him in his eyes. As he stepped around Vest to leave the club Rain Arsenal told him. "The bigger you are I'm gonna make sure your fall is hard as hell, so remember I warned you both I'm out."

Big Vest steps into Shelly's office to see her re-strap her *12*-gauge back to her desk. "Boss lady, just give me the word and I'll break Arsenal's neck!"

"Due time Vest, in due time."

*   .   *   *

Arsenal jumped into his Mercedes Benz CLE and pulled out his cell phone and dialed Trigger's number while starting the Benz. "Trigger, where are you?"

"Shit, me and Shotgun are over here at club US. Just chilling, and you know I came over to check on my bitch Night, fine ass," Trigger said while slapping Night on the ass.

"Cool, stay there, I'm on my way over, I need something done," Arsenal said as he hung up his phone and smashed out of the club Rain's parking lot.

Chapter 15

Shelly watched as Arsenal pulled out of the parking lot on her TV monitors as she reached for her crutches that were behind her desk. Shelly thought in her mind about some of the things that Arsenal was saying. Deep down in her gut she felt that something terrible was about to go down. In her head, she told herself to call her cousin Marcus to pick his brains because she figured if anyone knew anything it was him.

Marcus was still in the streets, he might not have been an active T-Y-L member anymore, but he was still knee deep in the streets. Using her crutches, Shelly made her way out of her office into the front of the bar. Where she saw a small crowd and Big Vest behind the bar playing host to some plus size woman. Shelly laughed to herself when she saw him trying to juggle two bottles of Cîroc and dropping one on the floor breaking it into a million pieces.

Big Vest saw her out of the corner of his eye and ran to her side. "Boss lady, what are you doing? You need to rest that foot, you know that." Vest told her as he tried to assist her.

"Vest, would you stop, I'm ok and I'm not handicapped. Would you go back over there and entertain big mama and them?" Shelly directed nodding her head in the plus sized women direction. Big Vest just looked at Shelly. "Look Vest, the only thing I'm about to do is check that blind spot and figure out where to put the camera. Now go." Shelly told him threatening to hit his big ass with one of her crutches.

"Ok boss lady, if you need me I'll be at the bar."

"And by the way, the one on the right is really cute." Shelly told him as she hopped her way into the blind spot.

Once inside the blind spot Shelly looked up towards the ceiling and corners. She had just figured out the place she wanted to put the camera when she heard a low beeping noise coming from the back corner of the blind spot. Shelly used her crutches to limp towards the beeping noise that got fainter as she approached. As Shelly made it to the far corner she looked down to see a cell phone. She had to use her nice size butt to scoot down the back wall to pick up the cell phone.

The cell phone beeped one last time before it went completely dead inside her hand. Shelly used crutches to get up off the club's floor that still had blood and broken glass on it. She made a mental note to herself... *"I found the place I need to hang up the camera, but now I got to find out who's fucking phone is this, and find the motherfucker to put up the camera, and to clean the fuck up back here. Maybe it belongs to that sexy nicca who came to a bitch's rescue..."*

*   *   *

DP opened the blinds in the master bedroom to let the sun's bright rays shine in. DP stared at Flower who was laid across the king size bed naked as the day she came into the world. DP thought to himself before going over there and giving her a light slap on the ass... *"Damn ma is fine and her sex game is off the chain, but she's not a first lady type. So, this will be it for her..."*

When DP smacked her on the ass, her right cheek stood still while the left one moved up and down like the

85

ocean. Flower stirred up out of her sleep and smiled at DP. "Yes daddy."

DP told her, "Rise and shine sexy. Go take a shower and get yourself together so I can drop you off, I got some things I need to take care of this Monday."

Flower set up in bed. "Daddy, how about you go take care of whatever you need to take care of and I'll stay here and clean up for you, plus I can cook a mean pot roast. Then after dinner I can give you some dessert," Flower said in her sexiest voice.

DP was always a person who meant what he said and said what he meant. DP turned his back on Flower as he started to leave the room, "Shower and I'll be downstairs waiting to drop you off in *15*-minutes and the clock starts now." Was all Flower heard him say as he walked out of the room.

DP was dressed in an all-white Roc Rev fit with some *95*-Air Maxes with a black Roc belt around his waist. He was in the kitchen drinking a glass of milk when he heard the side door opening. Not knowing who it might be, he grabbed the first thing he saw which was a king size iron.

When Butter turned the corner, he saw DP with the iron ready to strike. "Damn DP hold up, it's me big homie," Butter said with his hands held up to block the iron just in case DP swung it laughing.

"Shit, I didn't know who was walking in this bitch, just on point, you feel me?" DP stated setting the iron back on the kitchen counter.

"Hell, if you would have answered your phone you would've known I was on my way over," Butter said laughing and lightning a blunt that was stuck behind his ear.

"Butter, I think I dropped my phone at the club when I had to..." DP stopped himself because he had to remember that Butter didn't know what had gone down.

Butter looked at DP and said, "What big homie, when what went down?"

"Nothing Butter, I just need to swing by that club to see if anybody turned it in."

"DP you can forget about that, don't no motherfucker turn in cell phones," Butter said laughing and choking off the strong Kush at the same time.

"Butter it won't hurt to check."

Butter flicked the blunt ashes in the sink. "Yo' time, yo' dime. Anyway, I just left Kirkland and he said to come by he got that for you." Butter had just told DP when he heard Flower coming down the stairs. "Damn bitch you still here, my boy DP must have worn that pussy out," Butter said laughing.

Flower smiled at Butter while giving him the middle finger. "Forget you Butter. BP baby I'm ready," Flower said to DP with a big Kool aid smile on her face.

DP looked toward Flower and Butter while grabbing the keys to the Jag off the kitchen counter. "Change of plans babygirl." Hearing this Flower's eyes lit up like Christmas lights in December.

Butter, not one to miss a beat, caught the look on her face and cracked a joke. "Damn bitch. My main man tells you there's a change of plans and yo' pussy get soaking wet that fast huh?" Butter cracked still laughing while dropping the roach of the Kush blunt in the sink.

"Shut up Butter with yo' messy ass dang," Flower said hoping DP had a change of heart and was gonna stay another day with her to pipe her down.

When DP spoke, Butter's smile quickly turned upside down and Flower's did also. "The plan is, Butter here gonna take you where you need to go. While I go, take care of what I need to take care of."

"Damn DP, fam that's how you do a G? Leave me stuck with this bitch after you got yo' rocks off."

"Fuck you Butter, with yo disrespectful ass!" Flower said with her arms crossed in a pissed off stand.

DP walked over and gave her a quick peck on the cheek. "Dig shorty, leave yo' number with Butter because at this time I don't have a phone and I'll give you a ring when the time is right." Was all DP said before leaving the two in the kitchen to fuss amongst themselves.

Chapter 16

Arsenal pulled up at club US and to his surprise, it wasn't that many people there as he walked in. Arsenal saw Trigger and Shotgun at their favorite booth with Night, Trigger's main hoe and some thick white stripper. Who was getting all Shotgun's one-dollar bills as he made it rain on her while she popped her ass all on his midsection.

"What's good hood?" Trigger asked Arsenal as he slid in the booth with them and grabbed the bottle of Seagram's Gin and took a big sip from it.

Arsenal had to take a deep breath before answering him, because the Gin was so strong. "Shit, lover boys, but get y'all bitches to go chase dollars somewhere else while I put this bug in your ear," Arsenal said while taking another sip of Gin.

Night knew who Arsenal was and didn't take no time getting up and doing what she was told. Now on the other hand Pearl being new to the club didn't. All she knew was that this nicca came and messed up her cash.

"Listen homeboy me and daddy here," Pearl said while grabbing Shotgun's dick and kissing him on the cheek, "Are doing ok, so if you don't mind I think I'll stay a bit."

Before she knew it, Arsenal had grabbed her by her blonde hair and brought her face to his. "Listen bitch, if you don't get yo' funky ass up out of here. The nicca you calling daddy there," Arsenal pointed his finger at Shotgun. "I'm gonna have him slap the white off yo' ass and make you give them dollars back. Now get yo' thot ass the fuck out of here bitch." Pearl felt it in her gut that he meant business so she got up and got the heck out of there A.S.A.P.

"Ok Arsenal now that you scared our pussy away, what you got up your sleeve, my dawg?" Shotgun asked while grabbing the bottle of Gin off the table to take him a sip.

Arsenal looked around to make sure nobody could hear what he was about to lay down on two members out of his crew. "This the B.I., I just left club Rain hollering at the bitch Mz. Shelly about the takeover. And the bitch had the nerves to turn me down and on top of that, tthe bitch pulled a *12*-gauge and pointed that shit right in my face."

Shotgun had just taken a sip on the Gin when he spit it out after he had just heard what Arsenal said. "Bitch did what my nicca?"

Arsenal took the Gin from him and took another sip, "Yeah, Shotgun it's true." Arsenal told them while looking back and forth at the both of them.

"So A, what the fuck or should I say who the fuck you want nailed to the cross?" Trigger asked him while grabbing the bottle of Gin out of Arsenal's hand.

"Like I told the hoe Mz. Shelly, whoever ain't with the T-Y-Ls are against us, including her and her big fucking guard dog Big Vest."

Shotgun took the bottle from Trigger and took the last sip out of it before slamming it down on the table. "So, A, let the games begin."

"You damn right Shotgun, let the fucking games begin. I need for you two niccas to catch Big Vest punk ass and give his Shaq looking ass the blues and I'll take care of the ho Mz. Shelly," Arsenal said before getting up and leaving club Rain.

Outside in the parking lot he called Baby Nine.

"Hello?"

"Baby Nine, I need for you and Clips to turn up the heat in the streets, on all the dope boys, especially that nicca who goes by Butter. The streets talk and I've been listening…"

That was the last thing Arsenal said before hanging up his phone and smashing out the parking lot.

*   *   *

DP finally made it to club US after getting lost three times. He was greeted at the door by one of the big bouncers. Big Vest remembered DP from the other night.

"What's up playboy? I see you came to cash in on those free drinks huh?" Big Vest asked him after giving DP a man hug.

DP looked Vest up and down and swore he saw this dude in one of FP's pictures back in the joint, but pushed that thought out of his mind. "What's good, big guy? Naw, I just came here to see did anybody turn in a cell that I lost here the other night."

"A cellphone? I don't think people turn in cells anymore nephew but come on in and have a drink while I go and talk to boss lady and see if she knows anything." Big Vest told DP while escorting him to the bar.

Once at the bar Big Vest told Gracie, one of the daytime bartenders to pour DP a triple shot of Grey Goose. "Gracie do me a favor and pour…" Big Vest stopped dead in his sentence and looked at DP.

DP took this as a sign to tell the big homie his name. "DP is my name."

"Ok DP, I got you, playboy. Gracie, can you give DP here a triple shot and keep them coming while I go to the back and talk to Mz. Shelly."

"I appreciate it, big guy." DP told Vest as he took a seat at the bar.

Big Vest turned to him. "It's all good DP, it's the least I can do for what you did a few days ago. So, what I'm saying is, it's all love coming from this way. And you can call me Big Vest or Vest," Big Vest said before going to the back to talk to Shelly.

*   *   *

Shelly was on the phone with the company who installed her cameras throughout the club, when she heard Vest knocking on her office door. "Yes, I need someone to come out immediately to club US to install a few cameras inside my club. Yes, this is the owner. I dealt with y'all before, for this club and my other club, Rain. Yes, I'm satisfied with what I have, just need a few more installed for a couple of blind spots that were overlooked. Sure, no that's no problem. Yes, tomorrow will be fine. Ok 10:30 am, see you then."

Shelly hung up the phone and told Big Vest to come in. The whole time she was on the phone, her eyes were glued to the TV monitor in her office. She saw when the Jag pulled up in the lot and when the driver got out, it was hard to pinpoint who he was but Shelly had a feeling she was about to find out. "Come in Vest."

Big Vest entered the office to see Shelly rubbing her propped up ankle. "What's good boss lady. Your Superman is here," Big Vest said with a reading smile on his face.

"My Superman? Vest what is your big ass talking about now?" Shelly asked with an eyebrow raised.

"You know lil sis, o'boy who came to your rescue the other night. You know the pretty boy with the hands," Big Vest said with the biggest grin on his face.

At that moment Shelly knew what Vest was talking about, her knight and shining armor. "So what Vest, he's here to cash in on his free drinks I offered him anytime he's here?" Shelly asked Big Vest who was still standing in the office's doorway with that silly grin on his face.

"Don't know boss lady. I got him sitting at the bar with a drink in his hand. He told me that he would like to have a word with you."

"ME!"

"Yes you."

Shelly told Vest to give her *10*-minutes and send him in.

"Ok boss lady, will do," he said before closing the door.

Shelly took her makeup mirror out of her desktop drawer and looked herself over as she thought to herself... *"I was wondering when Mr. Out of nowhere to save a bitch ass was gonna drop by."* Shell had just put her makeup mirror away when Big Vest was knocking back on the door. "Come in Vest."

When Vest introduced DP, Shelly couldn't help but notice that he was much sexier then she remembered. She was just glad she gave herself a once over before this fine hunk of a man walked into her office.

"DP this is Shelly, boss lady this is DP, your hero," Big Vest said before closing the door behind him.

DP took one look at Shelly and just knew he had to get to know everything about this beautiful woman.

Chapter 17

After Butter dropped Flower off, he made a call to Brick.

"What's popping Butter?" Brick answered his phone on the 3rd ring.

"This what's popping Brick, I need for you to call the team and all you motherfuckers meet me at the house on the southside. It's time we check up on these chomps the T-Y-L faggots," Butter said before hanging up his phone and jumping on the highway headed towards the south to meet up with his team.

Butter knew that things were about to get hotter than fish grease, so for now, he decided to keep DP at bay just for now. Seeing that the big homie just got out after doing *10* years for his mishap.

*   *   *

So, Mr. DP, what can I do for you? If you're here to cash in on those free drinks, the bar is back out that way." Shelly told DP and used her well-manicured hand to point towards the office door that leads back to the bar.

DP cracked a smile that showed off his deep dimples that were implanted on both sides of his face. Seeing this, Shelly had to adjust herself in her seat because her lower body parts were starting to heat up.

"I don't mean to disturb you umm Mz. Shelly. First off, I wanted to see how you were holding up from the other night. Yo' team rushed you out so fast that night I didn't get the chance to see you."

Hearing DP being concerned about her just had Shelly feeling all warm on the inside. The only men that care about her well-being was Big Vest and her brother, and they both were family. So, to have this handsome man worried about her, had Shelly feeling some type of way. "I'm doing much better thanks to you, if you didn't come alone ain't no telling what would've happened. So, I do truly thank you DP," Shelly said with her sexiest smile on her face.

"No thanks needed Mz. Shelly, I'm just glad I was able to help. Besides, it's my duty to help a woman as beautiful as yourself." He told her while getting lost in her big round eyes.

Shelly let out a small cute laugh, that had DP wanting to hear that for the rest of his life. "OK DP, now what can I help you with?"

"Oh yeah right, well Mz. Shelly"

"Shelly, just Shelly is fine."

"Ok then Shelly, I dropped by to see did anyone turn in a cell phone that I happened to misplace the other night here. I figured I must have dropped it when we were back there dancing with them pussy takers."

Shelly wondered who that phone belonged to and since the battery was dead when she found it, she didn't find the time to charge it up to see who it belonged to. Shelly opened the second drawer on her desk and brought out the phone she found in the blind space. "Will this happen to be your phone DP?" She asked him while leaning over her desk to show him the phone.

DP grabbed the phone. "It looks like mine, thank you."

"Well, you are welcome but the battery is dead, when you charge it up and for some reason it's not yours, keep it. Because once a phone is lost, nine times out of ten you're not getting it back."

"Will do, and thanks Shelly," DP said as he reached over the desk to shake Shelly's hand.

"No problem sir." She told him as they shook hands.

DP got up to leave and turned back to Shelly. "Shelly,"

"Yes."

"I was wondering if it would be too much if I asked you out on a date sometime."

"A date? DP is that the real reason you came here and is that really your phone?" Shelly asked him with a teasing smile on her face.

"Yes and No."

"Yes and No? Huh, what do you mean DP please explain."

"Well, it's like this, Shelly from the first time I saw you the other night I wanted to get to know you. And to be honest with you, that's how I stumbled up on you and them clowns the other night. Because I was coming your way to meet and greet with you when I saw you turn into that crawl spot. And well, you know the rest, plus, I needed my phone," DP said while holding up the phone Shelly had just passed him.

Hearing this made Shelly's heart skip a beat, she felt so connected to him and she didn't even know him. "I'll tell you what DP, if you think about coming to work for me as head of my security team, then I think it won't be a problem going on a date with you."

"Head of your security, what about Big Vest?"

97

"What about Big Vest, I got another club that could use somebody with hands like yours. So how about it?" Shelly asked him.

DP didn't need a job, little did she know. DP took a moment to think to himself... *"Head of security. Man, do I look like 'Day Day' from the movie 'Friday.' Laughing my ass off, you know what I need, something to do until I figure out what my next move will be. Plus, it will help me keep Butter at bay until I let him know that I'm not getting back into that life."*

"So, sir what's it gonna be?" Shelly asked him but deep down inside she was praying he said yes. It's been a longtime since she enjoyed the company of a man.

"Ok, I'll tell you what beautiful. You got yourself security," DP said before turning to leave.

Last thing he heard Shelly say was, "And you got yourself a date handsome."

DP walked back in front to where the bar was and said his farewell to Big Vest who embraced him when DP told him Shelly had offered him a job. DP jumped into his car and headed to see Mr. Kirkland.

Chapter 18

Shelly's phone rang as soon as DP pulled out of the parking lot. It was her aunt; Silencer mother.

"Hello TeTe, what have you been up to?"

"Not too good Shelly."

Shelly could tell by her auntie's voice that something was terribly wrong. "TeTe, what's the matter?"

"Well, baby I have been trying to find your number for the longest now. You know I'm getting up there in age baby and TeTe don't see that well."

"What's the problem TE?" Shelly asked for the second time.

"Well, baby I begged and begged that boy of mine to leave them streets alone. Now, my boy is dead, Shelly they killed him. Somebody killed my baby."

As she listened to her auntie go on and on, Shelly knew that her old crew and Arsenal had something to do with the death of her cousin. "Listen TeTe, I'll be in Madison in a few days to come and talk with you. Let me wrap up a few things here and I'll be to see you," Shelly said to her aunt before hanging up the phone.

Shelly sat at her desk in disbelief from the news she had just gotten from her auntie. As she sat there, Shelly couldn't help but relive the conversation she and Arsenal had before this. When Arsenal said, I'll learn just like my cousin, she should've had Big Vest snap his neck then.

*   *   *

Butter walked into his trap house on the Southside to see Brick, Ecstasy, Scale and Pyrex sitting around the kitchen table drinking and smoking while talking shit upon waiting for his arrival.

"What up God?" Brick asked Butter as they embraced in a manly hug.

"What's good, Brick?" Butter replied as he and Brick stepped back from each other. As he looked around the table he gave the rest of his team a head nod before sitting down at the head of the table. "Y'all probably wondering why I had y'all meet me here on the southside?"

Ecstasy was the first one to speak. "I got a feeling you're gonna tell us Butter baby," she said while giving him a wink of her eye.

"You damn right I'm gonna tell you motherfuckers. It's time we address the matter at hand."

"Which is what Butter?" Pyrex asked him.

Before Butter could answer Scale the hot head out of them jumped up from his seat.

"The matter at hand is yo' young dumb ass getting robbed by them chumps T-Y-L. That's the matter at hand fool, damn!" Scale said while slumping back down in his chair.

"Yes, that's it, Pyrex. I've been keeping my ear to the streets and the word is, them fuckers is planning to take all the ballers for everything they have. But we got a treat for their asses," Butter said while grabbing a blunt full of loud from Brick. After a few pulls of loud he passed it to Scales. "Here nicca hit this shit and let me finish before you jump up and get to acting crazy G."

"Ok Butter I got you," Scales said as he inhaled the thick smoke.

"Ok then team, I need you fools to have all y'all soldiers ready for the jump off. Anybody repping or screaming this T-Y-L shit, I want hot lead in their asses. I don't give a fuck who it is, if they're with that shit, they gonna get it, point blank period. You motherfuckers hear me, I want them dead, dead. We gonna chill out for a sec on hustling and deal with this shit first. Do I make myself clear?" Butter asked his team.

Everybody gave agreement with a nod of their heads.

"Good, let's get to it," Butter said before he dismissed them.

Brick was the last one to leave before he turned to Butter, "Say kid."

"Yeah Brick,"

"What about DP? What's his role, God?"

Butter hadn't figured that out yet. "I'm going to holla at him after a while, but for now I'm gonna let him chill seeing he's fresh home." Butter told Brick.

"Right, Right I feel you son, word. I'm out, peace God," Brick said before leaving.

*   *   *

DP finally made it to Kirkland's office. Once he made it off the elevator he was greeted by his longtime friend's receptionist.

"Hello sir, may I help you."

"Yes, you can tell Kirkland DP is here." DP told the receptionist before having a seat in one of the chairs that was placed around the lobby. *15*-minutes later Kirkland was escorting an up and coming D-boy by the name of Seany Pee, who dropped off money every month to

Kirkland for retainer fees just in case anything was to happen to him while he was doing his thing in the streets.

"DP."

"Kirkland."

"Come on in her boy," Kirkland said as he let DP walk in first as he turned to his receptionist. "Hold all my calls and appointments." He told her before closing the door.

DP turned to face a smiling Kirkland. The two stared at each other before DP broke out laughing.

"What's good big bro?" Kirkland broke out laughing too.

"You tell me lil bro. Why the fuck you just now coming to see me fool. I'm still yo' big brother, don't have me kick yo' ass," Kirkland said as he took a playful swing at DP before they hugged.

"Naw bro it wasn't nothing like that. You know that boy Butter had me ripping and runnin," DP said as he sat down in one of the chairs across from Kirkland's desk.

"I hear you but who is this Flower I have been hearing you been laid up with. Mr. Ripping and Running?"

DP couldn't help himself from laughing. "Big Bro you know *10* years is a longtime. So, you know I had to knock some chick back loose but forget all that big bro, I see you moved up in the world from that little closet you use to rent across town."

They both fell out laughing. Kirkland and DP weren't real brothers; they both grew up as best friends on the same block, but Kirkland chose to go to school and DP chose the school of the hard knock life. Even though Kirkland was a successful lawyer, all his success came from DP who was using drug money to put Kirkland through school. Kirkland promised to pay back and be DP's mouthpiece whenever he needed him, little did DP know, Kirkland was the reason he got so much time in prison. If it wasn't for DP working on his own appeal he will still be locked away.

Kirkland acted like he was happy to see him but deep down he couldn't stand the sight of him and had plans to get DP out of the picture for good.

"So, Kirkland, tell me some good news."

Kirkland hated to share his money. "Well, DP what's good is that you are home bro."

"Yeah, you're right about that but what I'm talking about is my cash. I need it, because I'm out of the streets for good," DP said while rubbing his hands over his face.

Kirkland knew this day was coming and his heart skipped a beat knowing he had to part with his money. "Ok DP give me a few days and I'll have it all ready for you," Kirkland said as he stood up from behind his desk to walk DP out. "So lil bro I'll be giving you a call when everything is ready."

DP stood up to leave, "A few days, ok. I'll be expecting a ring," DP said as he turned the knob on Kirkland's office door to leave.

"A few days DP. A few days and welcome home again but I need to get back to work, time is money." He told DP as they shook hands and DP walked back to the elevator.

Kirkland stood and watched until the doors closed on the elevator. Once the doors closed he turned to his receptionist. "Give me *20*-minutes and you can resume calls and appointments," he said before returning back to his office and closing the door.

Once inside, Kirkland picked up his phone and made a call on his private line.

"Ring, Ring."

"Yo."

"Look, I don't know what's the holdup but you need to get on your fucking job before I find somebody to do it and you." was all he said before slamming the phone down with so much force, he broke the desk phone in half.

Chapter 19

Two days passed and Shelly tied up some loose ends and was on the highway headed to Madison, Wisconsin to talk with her aunt about her cousin. To find out what exactly went down. It was almost two hours later when Shelly found herself on the Southside of Madison Park in her aunt's driveway. Shelly sat there for about five minutes before she finally exited her 750 BMW.

Shelly was dressed in an all-black Gucci outfit with the shoes, earrings, necklace, sunglasses and purse to match. Shelly limped to her aunt's porch and twisted the wires on the broken doorbell. A second later Shelly almost shedded a tear when her aunt Bertha appeared from behind the now opened door.

"Hello Tete."

"Shelly you made it, come on girl you're letting all my heat out."

Once inside, Shelly looked around and saw her aunt hadn't changed a thing since the last time she was there almost eight years ago. Bertha sat on the plastic covered couch when she motioned for Shelly to come and sit next to her.

Once on the couch she took Shelly's hands in hers. "So Ms.Thang, how have you been?"

Shelly let out a small giggle because ever since she could remember her aunt been calling her Ms. Thang. "Auntie, I've been ok but the main question is how are you doing and what happened?" Shelly asked as a tear slid down her face and couldn't stop her own tears from falling.

The two sat there crying for *10*-minutes before Bertha spoke. "Well child, I begged and begged that boy of mine but when God calls you home, he calls you home. Well, I talked to that boy before he headed up to Milwaukee. And I asked him 'Son if yo're going to get into trouble, stay home. You don't need to be running around in Milwaukee streets.'"

Shelly saw in her auntie's face that the tears were about to start again, so she gently squeezed her hands. "Please Tete, go on."

Bertha gave her a weak smile and continued. "Well, Ms. Thang, he looked me right in my face and gave me a kiss on the cheek and said, 'Mama don't stress, I'll be ok just going up there to see my old homeboys, nothing to worry about.'"

This time Shelly couldn't stop her aunt's tears as her own tears started back up as Bertha yelled, "Now my boy is dead, Shelly he dead!"

As her head fell onto Shelly's shoulder, she stroked her aunt's gray hair and whispered in her ear. "Don't worry Tete, his death won't be in vain, I promise you that." Those were Shelly's last words spoken between the two before Shelly got up to leave. "Ok Tete, I need to get back." She told her aunt as she gave her a hug and a kiss on the cheek before heading to her car.

Once inside the car she gave Big Vest a call. "Ring, Ring."

"Yeah, boss lady everything ok?" Vest asked when he saw it was Shelly calling.

"No Vest it's not, get ready to war with our old crew," she warned before hanging up the phone to head back to Milwaukee.

DP couldn't help to notice how strange Kirkland was acting but he pushed it out of his mind as he went to go see the dirty cop who was on his payroll. He gave him the heads up whenever one of his trap houses was about to get raided.

Mr. Jordan had been fired off the force before DP got released, for beating a pregnant white woman who spit in his face to the point she lost the child. Word on the street was the unborn baby was really his and the white chick was a hooker who exchanged sex with Jordan so she wouldn't go to jail for prostitution.

DP pulled up on Good hope, the 8500 block in front of Jordan's two-bedroom, rundown house and got out. DP had to jump to the 3rd step because the bottom two were missing. Up on the porch it was broken beer bottles and cheap smashed beer cans all around the porch. Before DP could knock on the screen door a drunken Jordan snatched it open, gun in one hand and beer bottle in the other.

"Who are you nicca, and what the hell are you doing on my damn porch?"

DP couldn't believe how rough the years had been to this crooked cop.

"Speak nicca!" Jordan said aiming his .45 at DP's chest.

"Come on Jordan, I know it's been *10* years, but how you gonna forget me? All the cash I put in your bank account, now put that shit away so we can talk and I figure out what I owe you for that last information you gave me," DP said.

Hearing something about money had Jordan focus his eyes on DP. "Well, son of a bitch, get yo' ass in here,"

107

Jordan said as he lowered his gun and stepped aside so he could allow DP to enter.

Once inside DP saw more beer bottles and cans, along with boxes of half eaten pizza. Jordan closed the front door and ushered DP to a small kitchen table.

"Come DP, have a seat."

DP had to remove a beer can that was crushed on the old chair that had a crate for a bottom. "So, Jordan, I see you've been living the life," DP said as he looked around the funky, foul rundown house.

Jordan knew he was being funny and didn't take kindly to it. "Cut the bullshit nicca, you said you got something for me. Well, give mine to me so you can get the hell out of here and I can get back to… what you were saying oh, yeah, living my life," Mr. Jordan said as he took a sip of his beer.

"First things first, I need some info."

"Info, info on what nicca? My ass been kicked off the force, so how the fuck can I give you information nicca? Tell me this."

DP felt himself start to get upset at the way Jordan was wording his words. "Listen, you drunk clown ass nicca, if you shut your damn mouth for a second, I can ask you what I need to ask you and get the fuck out of this pig pin you call a home."

Jordan knew that he was pushing it with DP, because before DP went in he was one who meant what he said and said what he meant. "Ok, DP ask away."

DP rubbed the stubble on his face before he continued. "Well, Jordan, if you can remember the last information you gave me. I want to know anything and everything about that day."

Jordan could remember that day like it was yesterday. "Well, DP, you know back then I had a lot of informants. But it was one that was strange, so I started to do my homework on him."

"What do you mean strange, Jordan?"

"Well, you know most informants only give up information only to save their rat ass in the long run."

"Yeah, and?"

"Well, DP, this strange one didn't have a record or shit, hell, matter of fact, this one was even smart. Not street smart but school smart. So, there wasn't any need for him to be an informant unless he was just doing his good Samaritan thing, ya' dig."

DP had a strong look on his face as his mind raced a thousand miles an hour. "No Jordan, I don't dig, tell me more."

"Well, like I was saying, this snitch didn't have a record or even a J-walking ticket. So, whatever he was doing, it was out of spite."

"So, tell me Jordan, who is this informant?"

Mr. Jordan took a sip of his lukewarm beer and let out a loud laugh. "Ha, ha, ha. You mean to tell me you don't know who I'm referring to?"

DP was getting tired of the games. "Listen, you old drunk, just get to the point before I do."

"No need for that DP, the person you're looking for is your lawyer Kirkland," Jordan said taking the last sip of his beer and tossing it into an overflowing trash can.

"Kirkland?"

"Yeah, Kirkland. DP he's the one who helped put you away."

DP couldn't believe his ears but deep down he knew Jordan was speaking the truth.

"And just for the record, he helped other drug dealers out by ratting on them and sending them to jail."

DP took out a wad of cash and tossed it on Jordan's living room table. "Take this money, clean yo'self-up and speak no word of this or me."

Mr. Jordan let out a little laugh as DP turned and left.

Chapter 20

The T-Y-L crew was causing ruckus all over Milwaukee. If you were getting any type of money you had to watch your back.

Butter had just dropped off DP's one-night stand Flower when he scooped up his little homie Pyrex.

"What's going on big homie?" Pyrex asked as he jumped in Butter's whip.

"Shit youngin, cooling, you know getting to this money that's it, that's all," Butter said as he passed Pyrex a loud blunt to light up.

"I feel you Butter, I feel you on that plus, I need to get back after I was caught slipping."

Butter and Pyrex sat in Butter's car listening to music enjoying their high when Butter saw a Lexus pull up across the street and saw a fine chick get out and walk in the corner store.

Thinking out loud Butter said, "Damn, who is she?" Mainly speaking to himself.

Hearing him, Pyrex turn into the direction Butter was looking when he saw Baby Nine exiting the corner store. "That's that Bitch!!" Butter heard Pyrex say before he jumped out of Butter's car, gun in his hand.

Butter knew shit was about to go down so he grabbed his .380 pistol that he kept in the inside of his car door.

*   *   *

"Baby Nine, stop right here at this corner store. We need more blunts and while you're in there grab me some rubbers so I can tear that ass up." Clips told Baby Nine as he broke down some old grandaddy weed on a CD case.

"Listen boy, Imma go get the blunts but as far as some rubbers, you can forget that cause you'll never get none of this wet, wet you tick of a man."

"Fuck you BN and hurry your fine ass up."

Baby Nine was about 2ft from her car when she saw Pyrex, the young d-boy her and Clips robbed at the gambling house on 11th street coming across the street, gun in hand. Baby Nine noticed the driver door swung open when she was reaching for her .9 when she heard "BOOM!!" and her Lexus driver's window shattered.

It was Clips busting his Glock right through her damn window.

*　　*　　*

Pyrex had just come around Butter's car when he heard the first shot. As soon as he raised his gun to let off a shot, three more bullets came from out of the Lexus. Two of the shots hit him in the chest dropping him right to the ground, gun still in his hand.

Seeing Pyrex hit the ground and his green Polo shirt turning a dark red, sent Butter into rage. He jumped out with blood in his eyes, .380 busting.

*　　*　　*

Baby Nine dropped the blunts she had in her hands to get her .9 out of the small of her back, but she was too late. The dude who jumped out of the driver's side of the

112

car the young d-boy was in, started shooting at her. Before she knew it, she was shot in the neck and laid on the ground; blood shot out of her neck resembling a fruit punch water bubbler. Clips seen Baby Nine hit the ground and crawled out the passenger side door.

*　　*　　*

Butter saw the sexy chick fall to the ground when a round out of his .380 found its way into her neck. Butter then pulled Pyrex to the passenger side of his car and put him inside and slammed the door. As he raced to the driver's side Butter let off a few more rounds at the guy he saw crawl out the Lexus to help the chick he had just shot before jumping into his whip and pulling off.

As Butter raced away from the crime scene, he looked over toward Pyrex and he just knew that his little homie had just passed away. Butter knew he couldn't take Pyrex to the hospital because cops would be all over him with questions, and seeing that he just shot someone knew that was a big no, no. Butter pulled out his cell and dialed Brick.

"Ring, Ring"

"Yo, what's good?" Brick answered his phone.

Butter made a left on 21st street and pulled in the alley then parked his car at one of his side chick's garage. "Brick, some bullshit just went down, Pyrex is dead, and I just shot a bitch. I need for you to come scoop me up on 21st street. Yeah, you know who house I'm talking about. But before you do, call the team and have them meet us at the house downtown in an hour. Don't tell them the news yet, I'll pull everybody's coat then," Butter said as he hung up his iPhone 12.

Butter walked around to the side where Pyrex was at and shook his head. "Damn, Lil P, damn."

Chapter 21

Clips let out some shots at the nicca who just shot Baby Nine as the car smashed off. Clips looked down at Baby Nine and saw the quarter sized hole in her neck. He witnessed and killed enough people to know that his right-hand chick was dead. He pulled out his phone and called Arsenal.

"What's up Clips?"

"A, they killed Baby Nine, they killed her A, killed her!"

Arsenal couldn't believe what Clips just said.

"Little nicca, it must be April first and I'm being April fooled because I know ain't nobody killed Baby Nine, what the fuck happened? Matter of fact, meet me at the trap now! And I mean now little nicca, now!" Arsenal screamed before hanging up on Clips.

Clips took one last look at his partner in crime and wiped the one single tear that escaped his now swollen eyes. As Clips hear the police and fire trucks in the distance he turns to leave and for the first time he sees the small crowd gathering around him and Baby Nine. Clips was just about to tuck his gun, when he heard one of the lookers say…

"Damn, somebody just shot a fine ass bitch, that's a waste of some good pussy."

As the onlooker gave his guy a fist bump, Clips stopped in his '95 air max track and turned to face them. "What the fuck you just say about Baby Nine fools?"

The onlookers were caught by surprise so they didn't say a word just stared at a swollen eye Clips.

"What, you punks are at a loss for words now, huh? Well, me too, so if that's the real case, Imma let my mouthpiece speak for me and I'm not talking about any lawyers fag!"

Clips aimed his Glock and shot the guy right through his forehead, the bullet left a small hole the size of a dime but when the Glock bullet exited the guy's head it exploded as his head hit the cement. It resembled a Jack -An- Lantern six days after Halloween when the Jack -An- Lanterns are rotted out sitting on the curbside. The other onlooker seeing his guy getting shot tried to turn and run when Clips next bullet hit him in the back and flung him right into the streets where an Uber car hit him and sending him 8ft in the air.

When the guy came down his body was all twisted up like he was playing the old color game Twister by himself. Seeing his work was done Clips tucked his Glock and ran through a gang way to meet up with his T.Y.L crew.

*   *   *

The streets of Milwaukee have never seen such violence and such disregard for human life. Fox 6 news warned people to stay in their home, due to the fact that all the shootings that rang out all over Milwaukee. Every night it was so many shootings that the state of Wisconsin had to call in the National Guards, which still didn't help.

Arsenal wanted the heat turned up since Baby Nine got killed and that's what his T-Y-L crew have been doing, not sparing anybody. Clips losing his right-hand female was over the top and he didn't care who you were, old lady, teacher, preacher it just didn't matter to him. Clips sat in his '77 cutlass with twin Glocks in his lap smoking on some Kush sitting on the corner of 3rd and North scooping out club US for any and everybody he could release his anger on.

Clips turned down his *$2,500* sound system which was blaring out N.B.A Young-boy new mix CD when he saw Big Vest Hummer pull in the club parking lot.

"I knew I'll catch this ex T-Y-L trader sooner or later, now I got his ass right where I want him," was all Clips said as he smashed out his Kush and gave his twin Glocks a kiss of death as he jumped out of his tricked out cutlass.

Chapter 22

It's been going on three months since Shelly gave him the news about Silencer getting killed and they both knew who was behind it. Shelly has been deep in her thoughts and hasn't been making her normal runs and that's why he found himself making the money runs that she normally does.

As Big Vest entered the club he was greeted by DP, which he has been a great addition to their small family. "Dp how is it going?" Big Vest asked DP as they gave each other the pound handshake.

"You know Big Vest, same-o same-o this way, nothing new just the same horny dudes giving their hard-earned money away to these strippers." They both gave a laugh. "So, what brought you down here? Shelly normally comes in and picks up last night's take." DP asked Vest as they sat down in DP's private booth where DP poured him a shot of his Remy.

Big Vest killed the Remy and pulled out his costly cigar. "Well, to keep *1000* with you DP, Boss lady got a lot on her plate, past life, feel me. But nothing to worry about DP. Boss lady is built to last so she'll jump back like uncut coke."

Big Vest and DP sat around for about *20* minutes just shooting the shits. Big Vest was enjoying DP company so much that he tipped a few strippers before he got up to go in the back to get last night's money to drop off at the bank in the morning. Big Vest came out the back with *$11,000* tucked inside a Nike bookbag. He stopped at DP's booth to say his goodbye.

"Well, lil brother I got to make a few more runs so I'm about to disappear like last year." Big Vest told DP as he gave him a fist bump.

DP stood up as they fist bump. It was about 6:30pm and the strip club only had a few tippers around, mostly the normal. "Hold up Vest, I'll walk out with you, about to check out the lot and have me a smoke," DP said as he followed Big Vest out of club US.

*   *   *

Clips stood two cars behind Big Vest's Hummer with blood in his eyes. Only thing that kept replaying was Baby Nine getting killed. Clips wanted blood and that's what he was gonna get. He pulled out his Glocks and both had *30* rounds extendos when he saw the club lights emerge from the club as the front door swung open.

He told himself... *"This for you BN paybacks a Bitch!!"*

*   *   *

Big Vest gave DP one more fist bump as he headed to his Hummer. Vest was almost to his truck when he stopped and turned back towards DP. "Say DP."

"Yeah, Big Vest?"

"You should give boss lady a call, maybe you can bring her back around sooner, you know," Big Vest said with the biggest Kool aid smile on his face.

DP had just pulled the last hit off his cig and dropped it to the ground and smashed it out with the heel of his shoe when he heard the first shot.

"Boom!!"

*   *   *

Butter stood in front of his team, giving them the news about the youngest member out of their crew. "Listen, you motherfuckers and listen well." Butter told them with a 'I mean business tone' in his voice. "Pyrex..." was the only thing that came out of his mouth before he slammed his fist into the glass Scarface poster hanging over the fireplace in his downtown condo. Butter hand had minor cuts on it that he ignored. The blood from his cuts stained his carpet that Bumpy Johnson (the guy Denzel Washington played in the movie American Gangsta) couldn't pay a person to blot out.

Ecstasy, the only one out of the crew with tears in her eyes knew this time it wasn't Pyrex getting robbed, Jump up and said with a sad emotional tone in her voice. "No Butter, no..." Cause she had a female intuition that her little play brother was no longer walking this earth.

Butter grabbed a bottle of *1800* off his bar but instead of pouring him a shot he threw the bottle against the wall which shattered into a thousand pieces. "I need y'all to gather y'all soldiers and find these T-Y-L motherfuckers and send their asses back under the rock they crawled from up under. And I mean now, fast and in a damn hurry!" Butter said before he slumped down on his couch and covered his blood stain hand over his face.

Brick stood up and told the team, "Y'all, heard Butter, get out there and shake this city up kids. If they are not with us, they are against us and anybody against us is gonna feel us in the worst painful God forgiving way. Now go handle this B.I and I want all of you to report to me directly and I'll feel Butter in on the news y'all report to me. From this point on all, and I mean all drug sales STOP now!! It's war time, any money being spent better be on guns and bullets, son," Brick said to the rest of them. "Now Go."

Ecstasy was the last of them to leave the apartment when Brick grabbed her by her hand and stopped her right at the door when she was just about to exit. The touch from Brick hand started her tears to roll back out of her big pretty eyes. "Don't Brick, I must go, please don't try and stop me." Ecstasy told him without even turning around to face Brick.

Brick hearing Ecstasy words brought a sad feeling to his heart. Brick knew that of all the females he dealt with, E was the only one that really cared about him and he promised himself after everything was over with, he was gonna do right by her. Brick stepped around Ecstasy and used his big hand to ease her face up to eye level with his. "Listen Ma, these kids don't stand a chance. You my shorty, I promise you imma keep you safe with my last breath in me." He told her as he gave her a kiss on her cheek.

Ecstasy couldn't take any more as she snatched her hand away from Brick to cover her face as she ran to the elevator crying her pretty little eyes out. Brick couldn't help himself as he stared at her nice round ass jump up and down as she ran away with tears in her eyes. Brick just said "Damn…" as he closed the door and locked it. He turned around to see Butter back at the bar pouring up two glasses of Patron.

Butter gave him a glass as he killed his and poured him another before he spoke. "Brick, you my main man."

"That's right son," Brick said as he took a sip of his Patron.

"I need for you to be my eyes and ears like always. This shit just got real, real. You handle the team, everybody goes through you and you alone. I need to get my thoughts together and try to make sense of this shit here." Butter told Brick as he passed him a backwood of an old granddaddy Kush.

Brick inhales the weed smoke deep just so he can try and calm his nerves. "Say kid, what about the old head DP and what's his part in this?" Brick asked Butter as he passed the blunt back to him.

Butter hit the blunt then told Brick. "Imma go holla at him but I know he's gonna be on deck like some cards. Meantime, you go out there and see what you can kill my nicca," Butter said before he grabbed his car keys and his Glock .40 and headed to the front door to go find DP.

As Butter was closing the door he heard Brick say, "I got you son, killing is my middle name God!"

*   *   *

Hearing the first shot DP Sprung into action. Reaching in the lower part of his back DP pulled out his 9mm while at the same time yelling at Big Vest. "Vest lookout, get down, down Vest down!!!"

Big Vest was a little too late to react because after hearing the first shot Vest would never know how many more would come after that.

*   *   *

122

Clips saw his opportunity when Big Vest turned around to say something to the guy he walked out of the club with. Clips pulled out the Glock and took aim.

"Boom, Boom, Boom…" the shots were coming so fast and rapid it kinda put you in the mind of Nick Cannon when he was playing the drums in that movie 'Drumline.' Clips saw Vest slam against a new four door Tahoe. Big Vest slammed so hard into the truck that he put a dint in to the Tahoe's driver door and broke the window. Seeing this Clips let out four more shots.

"Boom, Boom, Boom, Boom…"

All the shots found their mark. Big Vest slid down the Tahoe right on his ass, gasping for air. Clips with rage in his heart and blood in his eyes wanted to over kill Big Vest for his partner in crime Baby Nine. He started to move in on his victim to unload the rest of his hollow point bullets into him, when Clips heard shots coming his way from the guy Vest was talking to a few minutes ago.

*　　　*　　　*

DP returned fire as he ran towards Big Vest.

"Pop, Pop, Pop, Pop…"

As DP was running towards Vest he could see sparks coming from the attacker's guns. From an onlooker, one would think that it was the 4th of July and some kids had two sparklers in their hands and were waving them back and forth.

DP let out a few more shots as the shooter he was aiming at turned the corner and was gone into the night. DP looked down at the big man Vest and he could tell he was trying to tell him something. DP got down on one knee and rested his hand on the destroyed Tahoe with his 9mm still pointed in the attacker's direction just in case he decided to double back.

Big Vest was trying to speak but it was hard for him to do so due to the fact he was gargling up blood from many bullets that were lodged into his body. DP leaned in close so he could try and make out whatever Vest was trying to say. When Vest tried to speak his words came out in the form of a huge blood spit bubble that popped in a spattered DP in his face. With one hand resting on the Tahoe and the other holding the pistol DP was all outta hands to wipe the spattered blood off his face. This time when his new-found friend spoke the words came out clear enough that DP could make out what he was saying.

Big Vest grabbed DP pants legs with his big hands and told DP. "You got to get to the boss lady, boss lady gone, need you..." was all that came out of his mouth before he took his last breath. DP looked Vest in his eyes and knew he was dead.

DP got off his one knee and finally noticed all the clubbers running in all types of directions. Far off in the distance you could hear the faint sound of sirens and that was DP's cue to get up out of there and find Shelly. DP turned and saw the second in charge security guard coming his way.

"DP, oh shit Big Vest. Man, what the fuck happened?"

DP finally got up from his crunch position and faced Soda-Pop, the man who was under him and running the security team at club Us. "Listen Soda, no time to talk just listen."

"Ok, DP I'm all ears."

"I need you to lock this bitch up. Make sure everyone is out then I need for you to take the tapes from the video cameras and get rid of them and I mean destroy them. Let the cops know that this was Big Vest's club and he was picking up the money to deposit it into the bank when he was robbed and shot."

While saying this DP reached down and grabbed the bag of money that his new dead friend had. DP reached in and gave Soda-Pop *$2,000* dollars. "Soda, take this, this should hold you off till you hear back from me."

"Love," said the second in charge of the security.

DP knew that the club would be swarming with cops any minute. "Look I got a dip, I'll give you a call and let you know when to open back up," DP said as he turned to leave. He stopped in his tracks but didn't turn around as he spoke to Soda. "One more thing Pop, I was never here," he said before jumping in his Jaguar. He started his car up with a push of a button and the Jag came alive with the headlights glowing like cat eyes in the jungle at night when it's on a hunt for food. And that's what the engine sounded like as it growled when DP turned out of the parking lot of club US to go find Shelly.

Chapter 23

Clips jumped in his tricked-out ride and sped off. Resting his 2 Glocks on his lap, he picked up his cell and called Arsenal.

"Ring, Ring…"

"Yeah, lil nicca, wait, you calling again to tell me someone else in the crew is dead? If so kill your damn self because I don't want to hear that shit," Arsenal said.

"No, A listen."

"Listen to what? What the fuck you got to tell me, and this shit better be better than sex with yo' mama lil nicca."

Clips laughed because he knew Arsenal and his mama was bumping and grinding back in the day. "Damn, A you a funny dude, but I'm calling to let you know that the Big nicca Vest is no longer with us, he's with Kobe Bryant playing center as Shaq in hell," Clips said before hanging up and looking for his next revenge.

He grabbed his blunt and thought back to the club shooting. "Name or no name, that fool who shot at me is next on my list, fuck it potato batata nicca gone die," the young killer said who's looking for revenge for his dawg in crime Baby Nine.

*　　　*　　　*

Kirkland knew things were heating up fast and he must get out of dodge before the flames catch up to him. He was sitting in his office destroying all files, papers, notes, anything that had his name on it. He pushed the safe button under his desk and the wall safe opened up. Kirkland started taking the money and drugs he had stashed in the wall safe out when he heard his office door creep open. He figured it was his receptionist and she must have come back early from her lunch, which he didn't mind because she could help him clean up the place and get rid of anything that could incriminate him and his malpractice of his law firm.

"Linda, I'm glad you came back early, look this is what I need for you to do. All paperwork, etc, shred it, deleted all files and disc and everything; just get rid of it no time for questions just do what I ask please, thank you!"

When Kirkland didn't hear his receptionist, Linda respond he came out of the wall safe and his eyes were bigger than a toad. "Wait, who the fuck is you?" Kirkland didn't recognize the big guy standing in front of him. Kirkland kept a loaded .25 handgun in his top office desk drawer, only thing he was standing at the wall safe so he had to figure out a way to get to it.

"Wait, if you want money it's none here. This is my office. I can give you my bank card with the pin and you can take all you want." Kirkland just stared at the man before him wondering why he hasn't spoken a word yet. The lawyer kept talking as he tried to inch his way over to his desk to grab his weapon when the intruder before him spoke.

"Stop moving!"

Kirkland stopped dead in his tracks. "Ok, I'm not moving but what do you want? My receptionist will be back any moment so you just better leave if you don't want to go to jail," Kirkland said staring the man down in front of him.

"Oh, she's back! She's at her desk tied up on the phone, one might say."

"Well, you better leave before the cops come because she knows to contact them anytime someone shows up unannounced."

"Fool, I said, she tied up on the phone, I never said she was using that motherfucker, it's different nicca. Now shut the F up and let me tell you something. See, I know all about you and how you been fucking people over with this law firm."

"I don't understand what you mean sir."

"Nicca cut the bull shit." The man looked towards the wall safe. "So, I guess you just got all them bricks of raw from the judge, huh? You see, I was doing homework and I got an A+ on your snake ass. Therefore, you want be representing nobody anymore." At that moment the man pulled out a Glock .40 and shot Kirkland two times in the chest which slammed him against the wall right into the mounted moose head.

The horns of the moose stuck Kirkland in the back of his head. If his body slides down from his neck one would think his head was mounted on the wall with the rest of the rare hunted animal. The shooter then proceeded to the wall safe took all of his belongings. As he proceeded to leave, he passed the receptionist who he had slapped in the back of the head with his Glock .40 before he tied her up with the phone line and taped her mouth shut.

Just before he exited the front office he leaned over the desk where Linda was and shot her two times in the left breast. Then the shooter was gone like a thief in the night with Kirkland's drugs and money.

*   *   *

DP slammed down on his brakes and jumped out of the Jag at club Rain and busted right in the front door. He came in like a mad man. A few of the security team tried to snatch him up before they realized who he was.

"Get the fuck off me!"

The night time manager saw DP bust in the club and was right there when the security team realized who DP was and let him go. "DP calm down please, the club is packed and folks are starting to look. I'm not trying to get them riled up because we both know how crazy these niccas can get, and plus Big Vest not back."

Hearing Big Vest's name brought a certain small peace over him that he finally looked around the club and saw the many people enjoying drinks and dancing. Dudes were having conversations with the chicks who they thought they could take home for the night and have sex with.

Even though the club was packed, the V.I.P section was closed, so DP told Ken, the night time manager to follow him up there so they could talk and didn't have to shout over the music or the people. "Ken follow me up to the V.I.P."

"Lead the way."

Once there DP turned towards Ken. "Listen, Big Vest is dead."

Ken took two steps backwards. "Dead, what do you mean dead, how, wait, are you sure, my nicca? Because that's Vest, and that big nicca is harder to kill than Jason and Freddy. I remember one time…"

"Motherfucker shut the hell up."

"My bad DP, go ahead"

"Ok, long story short, the big homie came to club US to pick up the money, so we talked a bit so I decided to walk out with him to have a smoke. As he was walking away, some fool came out of nowhere and just got to blasting. I blasted back but it was too late. Next, thing I know, Vest is spitting up blood and telling me to go find the boss lady. She's gonna need my help. So here I am now, so is Shelly in her office?" DP had beads of sweat all over his face when he finally got done talking. He grabbed Ken by the shirt. "Ken where the fuck is Shelly?"

Ken came out of shock. "Sorry DP, but Shelly is not here, she had just called and said she'll be here in a second."

"Ok, give me that gun off your waist." Ken did what he was told and gave DP his gun. "Now listen, you are in control of the club, I'm going to wait in the parking lot because it's to many people in here, and right now I don't know who we can trust. But let the club go as planned until you hear otherwise," DP instructed before leaving out the club to sit in the parking lot to wait on Shelly.

Chapter 24

Shelly had a million things running through her mind. She exited off the freeway and headed right to the club Rain to talk with Big Vest about their next game plan. Because she knew deep down in her heart, shit was about to hit the fan and shit stank.

Shelly pulled right into her parking spot. She hit the push start button to turn off her 750 BMW. When she reached for her phone, it happened to slip out her hand and land on the floor of the BMW. She bent over to pick up her phone. As soon as she set up right DP was at her driver's door window with a worried look on his face that scared the mess out of her.

"Shelly, Shelly let down the window, down, down, Shelly down!!" Was all Shelly could understand coming out of DP's mouth.

*   *   *

DP was sitting in his car in the parking lot waiting on Shelly to pull up. Things were getting out of control and he didn't have a clue where the shit was coming from or where it was going. All he knew that he wasn't going to let no harm come to Shelly. He closed his eyes for a second to try and make sense out of the whole situation. As soon as his eyes reopened, he saw Shelly pulling up in her foreign car and parking it right in her spot.

DP wasted no time, he jumped right out of his Jag and ran up to Shelly's car window... "Shelly, let down the damn window!!" The only words DP was able to get out of his mouth before all hell broke loose.

*   *   *

Not really able to understand what DP was trying to say. Shelly went to push the button that controls her car window but there was no need to because Shelly's car window was being shot out by an unknown shooter. As soon as she went for the window button, her back and passenger side window was being shot out.

"Shit, who the fuck is shooting at me?" She screamed over the gun shots to DP, who was returning gunfire back in the direction of shots. He was shooting blind because he couldn't see anybody at all.

DP screamed at Shelly to start the car and jump over to the passenger seat because he was about to drive them out of there. "Shelly! Shelly!"

"Yeah, DP I hear you."

"Start this motherfucker and jump over to the passenger seat with your head down. I'm about to slide in and drive us the fuck up out of here!" He yelled loud enough to Shelly so she would be able to hear him over the nonstop gun firing.

"Ok!" Shelly said before doing what she was told to do by DP.

Once DP heard the big block engine in the 750 BMW come to life, he let off a few more shots before sliding into the driver's seat of Shelly's car and smashing off.

*   *   *

Trigger and Shotgun have been lurking around club Rain trying to catch Mz. Shelly slipping. "Damn Shotgun, this shit seems like a waste of my fucking time. Shit, I can be getting some money, some ass, hell, I can be giving food out to the homeless if I wanted to. But nooo, my fool ass is with yo' ass trying to catch the old boss bitch. All because she G checked Arsenal ass for trying to handle her rough." Trigger told Shotgun who was really not paying him any attention.

His attention was more on the figure that emerged out of the blue, not to far from Shelly's parking spot. Trigger was still going on about something when Shotgun told him to shut up.

"And another thing Shotgun, yo' ass supposed to be the mastermind out of the T-Y-L crew. Why don't your smart ass just figure out a word problem or math problem to make her ass pop up. You know 2+2=4 type shit because my legs hurt and my ass is getting hungry, shit I don't know about you but."

"Trigger will you shut the hell up something is about to go the fuck down." Shotgun told his motormouth homeboy. Trigger kept his mouth close long enough to zero in on what Shotgun was talking about.

"T, you see what I'm seeing?"

"Yes, my boy, but I can't make out if the nicca is friend or foe?"

Just then his question was answered, when Mz. Shelly pulled in her parking spot. The two T-Y-L members were frozen in their seats, they really didn't know what to do. So, they figured they would let the unknown shooter take care of business because they didn't want to have a three way shoot out not knowing who that person was.

"I'll tell you what, Shotgun pass me that bottle of gin, while I light this here Newport because my ass is about to chill and watch this shit," Trigger said as he lit his cigarette and took a swig of the gin.

Shotgun knew his homeboy had a good point. "Pass me that bottle motormouth and short me on that Newport 1000 fool." Shotgun told trigger as he adjusted his seat to get a better view of the situation that was unfolding.

Trigger gave out a little laugh. "Here, take the bottle but this Newport, shit you'll have a better chance of finding Nemo then getting a short off this cigarette." Trigger told his homeboy as he tossed him the box of cigarettes and told him to light his own.

They both gave out a laugh as they saw Mz. Shelly's car pulled out of the parking lot and the shooter disappeared like a dope fiend in the night.

"Well, well, well Trigger, that was some off the wall shit."

"I know what you mean playboy, but who the hell was that nicca is all I want to know?" He questioned as he took the bottle outta Shotgun lap to get him a swig.

"Yeah, T, I was thinking the same shit."

"You know Arsenal is about to have smoke coming out of his ass when he finds out some no-name shooter, let Mz Shelly get away with some clown ass nicca," Trigger said as he went back in the box of Newport's to light up another one.

"Yeah, I hear you Trigger, but hell, it wasn't our fault," Shotgun said facing his partner in crime.

"Man Shotgun, shut up because we both know if that no name nicca would've got the job done, we were gonna take the credit for that shit," Trigger said trying to get the chcap gas station lighter to light.

134

"You damn right we were Trigger, you know the saying no face no case but in this case no killer, then we're the killers." Shotgun had to laugh at himself.

"Hahaha..." Trigger was trying to tell him something but Shotgun couldn't figure out what his motormouth homeboy was trying to say. Due to the fact he had that damn Newport hanging out his mouth and it still wasn't lit yet. "Man, fool I can't understand yo' ass, here give me the cigarette and I'll light the motherfucker," Shotgun said as he took the cigarette out of Trigger's mouth and lit it with his own lighter.

Once lit, Shotgun hit it twice and passed the Newport to his partner. "Here fool, now what the hell were you trying to tell me?" Shotgun asked Trigger, who was just sitting there quiet not even reaching for his own cigarette. "Fool, Fool nicca what the hell is your problem, you got to shit or something? Trigger!! What the hell is your problem?"

Just when he was about to speak his head exploded and brains and skull pieces flew all over Shotgun. The so-called mastermind couldn't understand what the hell had just happened. He sat there in disbelief unable to speak or unpuzzle what was going on. Shotgun was turned to Trigger's half a head and face and didn't see the dark figure creep up on him.

"I hear you are supposed to be the mastermind out of the crew now, huh?" The silent killer spoke with pain in his voice. "And if that's the case, I figured you wouldn't mind a riddle/puzzle that I put together."

Shotgun spoke for the first time since seeing his partner's head blown off his shoulder. "And what kinda riddle/puzzle are you referring to, sir?" Shot asked the killer, still couldn't believe he let a nicca catch him slipping.

"You know the kind, the Humpy Dumpy kind. You gotta put your partner's face and head back together before he can sit on the wall again."

"You motherfucker!" Were Shotgun's last words before he was struck in the back of the head and dragged out the car.

Chapter 25

DP hit a few corners before he told Shelly she can get up from under the dash board. Shelly set up and just gazed out of the window with a blank look on her face.

"Shelly, Shelly, are you hit anywhere, are you ok?"

Shelly can see DP's lips moving but couldn't hear the words that were coming out of them. Her tears just got to running down her face. For the first time out of her life Shelly or Mz. Shellz didn't have a handle on the situation at hand. She turned to DP and wondered why God sent her an angel out of all the wrong she had done or committed. With all the excitement going on Shelly closed her eyes and drifted off into a well needed rest.

*   *   *

DP slowed the powerful BMW down to a reasonable speed. With everything going on, the last thing he needed was a cop to pull them over. He had a thousand thoughts running through his head and didn't know where to start or how to figure them out. He glanced down at the gun on his lap and thought to himself. *"Man, what the fuck is going on? Big Vest is dead, and some fool just tried to kill me and Shelly. And that's twice my ass almost got nailed to the cross. If I aint throwing bricks back at the pen then who the fuck is? If FP knew how I'm living and the shit I'm involved in he would blow a gasket and be disappointed in me. But hell!"* DP glanced back at the resting Shelly.

"He'll have to get over it and understand that it's something about Shelly that needs me to protect her from the world and everything that's in it..." DP thought as he headed to her beach house on the far Eastside. He figured that will be a good place to chill at until he can make good of the situation that they're in.

*   *   *

The silent shooter was pissed at himself for missing his mark. He had a job to do and he planned to get that job done by all means necessary. He promised himself the next time his aim will be on point. Plus, the guy who wanted his target dead was really starting to get on his nerves with the phone calls and threats.

"Fuck I can't believe I miss. I never miss from this range. I know what it was. It was them bad luck fools across the lot watching my marks. I should've taken their asses out first then came back for my intended mark. Because something tells me they were up to no good but for whom? Well, at this point it really doesn't matter because next time the more people that are around, more bodies will weigh up..." The silent killer thought to himself as he disappeared into the night.

*   *   *

Arsenal had been blowing up the main members' phones in his crew and wasn't able to reach anyone it seems. He needed to know the ups, the downs and all the rounds in the streets so he could know his next move, but he wasn't able to reach no one.

Arsenal dropped his phone in the passenger seat and cracked the window in his Lexus truck to blow out the Kool's cigarette smoke. He liked to come down to the lakefront and do a few lines of coke. Him doing coke at the lakefront always made him feel like nothing exists but him and him only. Arsenal had just brought his head up when the headlights of someone's vehicle blinded him to the point he threw his hands up to block the light causing him to knock all his coke down.

"Why the fuck these damn fools not answering their fucking phones. I need to know what I need to know. I'm Arsenal (The leader over the T-Y-L crew) when I call them, their ass supposed to answer." The coke had Arsenal slurring his words every time he brought his head up from doing a line of coke.

"Sniff, Sniff. And I know one thing, if you want something done, you gotta do it yourself. Aye! Turn them bright ass lights off shit! Motherfuckers made me waste my damn shit. Whoever driving that motherfuckeris about to know that I am Arsenal the fucking leader over the T-Y-L click. The baddest crew in the fucking Midwest."

Arsenal had to wipe his face and eyes so he could zero in on the vehicle that had made him waste his shit. When his vision finally cleared up, the coked-out boss couldn't believe his eyes. *"Wait a goddamn minute, oh hell naw, is this who I think it is?"* Arsenal thought to himself as he cocked the hammer on his 10mm. "Yeah, that's her, that bitch. Got yo' ass now and whoever that nicca is, Imma pop his ass just because he got the pussy before me." Arsenal laughed to himself as he tried to scrape up some coke off the car seat.

"Yep, it's lights out they ass. Sniff, Sniff," Arsenal said to himself as he got out of his whip.

*   *   *

After meeting with his crew and giving them the instructions on how to play things, Butter decided to pay his big homie a visit and put him up on things and the loss of Pyrex. Whoever these niccas were, they had to be stopped and Butter knew his big homie would have answer on how to go about getting it done.

After hitting DP on his phone with no answer, Butter decided to hit up a few spots where he thinks he might run into the OG. When Butter pulled up to the club Us he couldn't believe his eyes. "Holy Shit, what the fuck," is the words that escaped his mouth when he saw his OG blasting at someone peeling out the parking lot and heading who knows where. He tried the big homie phone one more time.

"Ring, Ring. Come on DP pick up, pick up the phone. Ring, Ring…" with no luck Butter just hung his phone up and put his car in drive and headed towards his house where DP had been living. "Damn still not picking up, Fuck!" He could be only headed to one place and that's my house. Guess we're both headed that direction then because I need to know what the hell is going on.

"First, Pyrex now, DP shit I can't take any more bad news…" Butter said to himself as he peeled off rubber as he exited the parking lot to try and find DP and get a must needed answer.

*   *

Brick just had been lurking around Milwaukee ghettos making sure his little soldiers were alert and ready. He had just dropped off some boxes of bullets and a few

140

handguns to his block soldiers on 2nd and North when he heard the gun battle up the street.

"Pop, Pop…"

"Boom, Boom…"

"Pop…"

"Boom, Boom…"

"Pop, Pop…"

"Boom, Boom…"

"Pop, Pop, Pop…"

"Y'all hear that shit young boys? See, that's what I am trying to tell y'all. Y'all got to stay ready, so y'all don't have to get ready, because them gunshots we hear around the corner, can be just as easy coming y'all way. So, here's more bullets and guns because I need for my youngins to be on point like icicles." Brick told the little shooters in front of him. "And once this shit is over, it's going to be more money for each and every one of you niccas, mark my words. We are the winning side and win we will do all around the board. Y'all boys just be easy." Brick told the foot soldiers in front of him as he took a sip of Remy and passed it to the baby gangsters, who passed it among themselves.

As Brick drove off to his next destination, he pulled up to the stop sign on 2nd and Center when Brick decided to take out his phone and call Ecstasy to make sure she was ok.

"Ring, Ring."

"Hello Brick."

"What's good Ma?"

"Nothing, just sitting here thinking about everything that's going on."

Before Brick spoke, he looked to his left and saw a group of grimy looking dudes staring his way. With

141

everything going on Brick wasn't taking any chances. He grabbed his .45 pistol and made sure it was one up as he laid it on his lap. "Yeah, Ma, I feel you queen. Tell you what E, how about you get dressed and I'll be there in a hot second to pick you up, so we can grab a bite to eat."

"Brick, are you sure? You know it's a lot going on," Ecstasy said.

"I'm sure Ma, just get ready because I'm on my way," Brick said before hanging up his phone.

He turned on his signal light going left to head up Center to pick up Ecstasy. Brick made it to 3rd and was stopped by the red light thinking to himself when out of nowhere his truck was hit.

"Boom!"

Brick truck was smack so hard, it rolled over twice before landing on top of a parked car at Lil Generals, the everything you need store. The red and black Kia that hit him was about 3ft from Brick on its side when Brick saw four figures trying to get out of the stolen Kia.

"Oh, hell fuck naw. These motherfuckers totaled my shit and think they about to bail out on me, the devil is a fucking lie," Brick said out loud to himself.

He used his legs to kick out the windshield on his Q7 truck. As he kicked out the window he heard one fleeing passenger say, "Come on G, they can't stop no Kia Boy, off to the next one," the car thief yelled as he hopped out the banged up stolen Kia and ran past Brick's crashed up Q7 on his getaway escape.

As the windshield gave way, the banged and bruised up Brick looked around for his weapon. He saw it lying not to far from his phone that was lightning up due to the fact it was Ecstasy hitting his line back, probably wondering where the hell he is at.

Brick snatched up his pistol and phone as he rolled out his torn-up truck. Phone in one hand, pistol in the other. "Hello?"

"Brick, where the hell are you? I'm getting hungry and my ass didn't get dressed for nothing you hear me, Brick?"

Brick was going off all adrenaline that he didn't feel the metal rod that came from the backseat and found its way into his top back exiting out his shoulder blade. Brick tried to raise his right arm to shoot at the car thieves while bringing his left arm up to answer his phone. "Hello E, yeah, I was on my way but them damn Kia Boys hit my truck, but no worries, I'm about to hit their ass with these hollow tips," Brick said as he tried to raise his gun arm.

Whole time Ecstasy was on the other end of the phone screaming Brick name. "Brick, Brick what's going on, what happened, who hit your truck? Please, Brick say something, Brickkkk!"

The whole time Brick could hear her calling his name but he was trying to figure out why his gun arm wasn't coming up to shoot at the now gone Kia Boys. That's when he happened to look down and see the metal rod hanging out his shoulder. "Fuck!"

"Brick, what's wrong, are you ok? Brick!"

"E, we might have to take a raincheck on dinner and you just meet me at the hospital." Brick manage to get out his mouth before he passed out.

As the phone dropped out of Brick's hand you could hear Ecstasy on the other end. "I'm coming, Brick."

Chapter 26

Shotgun awoke with both his hands and feet tied together. He was sitting in a metal chair in the middle of a room naked. Shotgun opened his eyes and tried to adjust to the dim light in the room. Once his eyes adjusted he tried his best to focus on his surroundings. *"Where the fuck am I?"* He thought to himself as he surveyed the captured room he was in.

As far as Shotgun could see the place had to be abandoned, because the windows had boards on them and the room he was in smelled of mildew and animal feces. Shotgun could hear running water in the distance. As he zeroed his eyes in that area, he saw a sink of some kind running over with water. *"What the hell is going on?"* The T-Y-L member said to himself as he felt the cold grit water slide in and out between his toes.

"Ok Shotgun, use your head to figure out the situation you're in." He told himself as he gave the room one more good look over. The only thing Shotgun could see is a bunch of electrical wires but couldn't see what they were connected to. As he continued to search the room he saw a small movement to his left. "Who's there, show yourself." The so-called mastermind out of the T-Y-L crew sat there ass naked waiting on a movement of some kind or a voice telling him the answers he was looking for. "Who the fuck is out there? Listen, listen whomever you are, help me get out of this damn chair. I can pay you, how much you want or need, just help me out." Still nothing but silence.

"Ok, listen to me you motherfuckers. I'm Shotgun the mastermind of the T-Y-L crew. You hear me? Listen, help me and I'll make sure your good deed doesn't go unnoticed. You hear me motherfucker, help me or when I get out of this chair Imma!"

"You gonna do what you say?"

Shotgun froze in fear as he saw the shadow emerge up out of the shadow itself. "Who is that?" Shotgun asked with beads of sweat popping out of his head.

The ghostly shadowy figure didn't speak as he stood behind the tied-up T-Y-L member.

"Aye, man what kinda freaky shit you got going on? Whatever it is, you can leave me the fuck out of it my dude."

The ghostly figure wasn't faded by Shotgun's words, as he placed a metal crown on top of his head. "Hold up playboy, hold the fuck up! Damn, let's talk a minute and come to some type of agreement."

With all types of different color electrical wires hanging from the metal crown on top of Shotgun's head, he looked like a player on the hit show 'Fear Factor.' Who's about to get sent home from not completing his fear factor test. Once the unknown stranger had firmly placed the home-made construction upon the kidnapped T-Y-L member's head, he grabbed all the wires in one hand.

"Say man, aye man, I know you can hear me. Listen, just stop what you're doing and hear me out."

The unknown stranger walked a few steps and dropped the wires he was holding onto a circuit board looking object, before he turned around to face Shotgun. "So, mastermind, I'm going to ask you a few questions and depending on your answer, will determine how many switches on this board get turned on," the stranger said as he went about hooking the wires up to the circuit board.

"Awww, fuck, that shit hurts."

"Sorry about that, it seems one of the small switches was on. Here, let me go through the circuit board and make sure they are all turned off, don't need any of the high volts switch turned on. You might not make it back from it," the stranger said.

Shotgun finally was able to catch his breath. "Man listen, ask me what you need to ask me, no need to turn that shit back on." Because of the metal chair and the water running around the chair, Shotgun could still feel tiny waves of electricity running from the top of his head to the bottom of his feet.

"In due time, in due time mastermind, the truth should set you free," the stranger said as he connected the last wire to the circuit board.

*   *   *

DP pushed Shelly's code into her private entrance to open the underground garage door to her beach house. Once inside, the doors come down when a vehicle rolls over the garage door cord. DP pulled right next to Shelly's Bentley truck and turns off the shot-up BMW. DP gave Shelly a light touch on her arm.

"Shelly, Shelly wake up!"

Shelly came to, almost not recognizing her own garage. "DP, where are we?"

"I brought us to your eastside beach house so we can try and figure out the God sake name is really going on. Big Vest is dead and we almost…"

Hearing her brother from another mother is dead brought Shelly loses it all. "What! Who is dead? Wait! No, noooo! DP please tell me this is not true, tell me now!" Shelly cried out as she continually punched on the BMW dashboard.

DP hating to see her in this state, reaches over and grabs her by her hands. "Shelly, please stop punching on the dashboard." He told her as the blood from her knuckle dripped through his fingers and made a small puddle on Shelly's black Gucci pants.

Not even looking at him, Shelly stared out the window with a blank hopeless look on her face. How loud Shelly words came out her mouth at this time, a deaf person could've heard her pain; and a blind person would have seen the hurt in her eyes as you got a glimpse of them every so often when her tears slowed down and right before they started back up.

"DP, I thank you for…"

*　　　*　　　*

"Ok! Please don't turn it back on. I told you all I know. Why are you still turning on those damn switches?" Shotgun asked the stranger.

The unidentified man just stood there looking at Shotgun, who was slobbering at the mouth, a mixture of blood and saliva, with green and red snot coming out of his nose. Shotgun was shocked so many times by the stranger that his skin was starting to peel off his body. His eardrum burst, his toenail and fingernails both had turned black and was just popping off his body. He had light smoke coming out his body and he smelled of burning flesh and rotting human remains.

"Well, my guy, it's about time I went about my way, since you say you have no more information for me." The stranger told the dying T-Y-L member.

Shotgun mustered all the strength and energy he had left in him, to hold his head up and try to focus his right eye on the stranger because his left eye had popped out the socket. "Yo, man you can't leave me like this. I'm dying, I need help, help me!" The dying T-Y-L member tried to say out loud, but only came out as a low faint whisper through his cracked, split and dry bloody lips.

"Huh, what was that? Did you say something? Hello motherfucker, well, I guess not," the stranger said as he hit the main power switch on the homemade circuit board, that powered all the switches to come on all at one time, as he exited the building.

Shotgun was jerking and twitching so hard he caused one of the high voltage wires to undo itself and fall to the base of his penis, causing it to swell up and split. It kinda puts you in the mind frame of a hotdog that has been boiled too long to swell and pop. Shotgun gave one more jerk and twitch before he passed on to the next life.

*   *   *

Scales bust in the hospital waiting room door like a mad man looking for Brick as soon as he got the call from Ecstasy. He was on his way ready for action.

"Brick, Brick, Ecstasy where the fuck are y'all?"

Scales was causing such a commotion that the hospital staff and security guards had him surrounded. "Sir please calm down or we are gonna ask you to leave the hospital grounds." One of the nurses told Scales while standing behind a fat security guard who looked like he just came from lunch because he had crumbs of bread in his beard and all over his security guard's vest.

"Sir, sir."

"Sir my ass, I'm not trying to hear any of that bullshit. If you motherfuckers don't tell me where my homeboy is, y'all gonna have to throw me out this bitch. So, let's go fatboy," Scales said as he pointed at the fat security guard while placing his back against the hospital wall getting himself ready just in case he got bum rushed by hospital staff.

The hospital staff was closing in on Scales fast when Ecstasy made her way through the small crowd. "Stop it, he's with me!" Ecstasy screamed at the staff who was just inches from throwing Scales out. The hospital staff gave out a few vocal warnings before they went on about their duties throughout the hospital.

"Scales."

"E, how is he now?" Scales asked Ecstasy as they parted from their hug.

"He just came out of surgery so he's resting now, but the doctor said he's going be ok, thanks to God." Ecstasy told Scales as she passed him a cup of coffee.

"That's good to know E. Aye, where is Butter at, he's not here when he should be. See that's the bullshit I am talking about. But don't trip, people just got to learn shit the hard way I see," Scales said as he threw the cup of coffee against the wall on his way out the hospital.

Ecstasy just watched Scales storm off but didn't really think anything of it because she was used to him and his temper. "That boy needs to get him some pussy," she said before going back to sit with Brick in the recovery room.

Chapter 26

As Arsenal was making his way across the lawn parking lot into the sandy beach area that entered into Shelly's private backyard when his phone rang.

"Ring, Ring…"

"Clips, where the fuck are you and everybody else?" Arsenal asked him as he dropped down to one knee with his hand covering up the screen on his phone to try and block out its light.

"I can't speak for everyone else but I'm at the same place you are. You see I have been following…"

Arsenal had to keep his voice down and try to keep the light from the phone covered while he spoke to Clips. "What little nicca, how you know where the fuck I am if you're one of the fools who haven't been answering their fucking phones when I been calling," Arsenal said to Clips while still down on one knee.

"Arsenal, chill big homie and look to your left by the rocks, yeah you see me in the cut like a band-aid. Told you I can't speak for the rest of the crew but I'm here on every corner like stop signs taking care of this business," Clips said as he made his way towards Arsenal.

*   *   *

"Ok, now that I got that out the way, plus the information I need, it's about time to wrap this shit up and take care of the last things that need taking care of." The unknown stranger thought out loud to himself as he descended the stairs two at a time to get as far away as possible from the abandoned house and all its deadly secrets that were left inside. As the stranger was walking away he pulled out a cellphone that he happened to pick up and dial a number that he saw in the contacts.

"Hello?"

"Yeah, I need a ride to the lakefront."

"Ok sir, your Uber will be there shortly."

Ten minutes later the stranger was tossing the cellphone away as he climbed into an all blue box Chevy Uber and was on his way.

*   *   *

Clips just stared at Arsenal as they set in Shelly's private backyard and he did a few lines of cocaine.

"Yo Arsenal, I don't think we have time for that shit," Clips said as he checked both clips on his Glock .40.

"Say listen youngin, we got time for what the fuck I say we got time for," Arsenal said as he snorted the last line of coke that was mostly lint balls and dirt that he scraped off the front seat of his car.

"So, boss, what's the plan and how do you want to play this seeing that it's only me and you here?" Clips asked while examining his Glock .40.

"Shit, lil nicca, what are you talking about? We're about to bum rush this bitch and everybody gots to go. Fuck you mean?" The leader of the T-Y-L crew said as he cocked his *10*-millimeter handgun and headed towards the beach house. With Clips in tow right behind him.

*   *   *

Butter was about to head to his house that DP resides in, but changed his mind when he saw him turn out of the parking lot of the club and headed further east.

"Come on DP, where are you headed to?" Butter had to ask himself as he saw DP make a right, then two lefts and pulled up to a nice size beach house. Knowing he didn't have the code to get in the private entrance that leads to the garage. Butter decided to park up front and figure out his next move.

*   *   *

Scales came through the double sliding doors at the hospital on ten and ready to take care of business. He took out his phone and dialed up Butter.

"Yeah."

"Butter, where the fuck are you?"

"I'm down on the east side and something just doesn't sit right with me." Butter told Scales as he parked in front of the beach house and got out to look around.

"Say Butter you tripping right now, yo' right hand man is sitting up in the hospital and you're fucking off on the trifling ass eastside, why?" Scales questioned as he jumped in his car and slammed the door.

"Look Scales, Ecstasy is keeping me updated on Brick and from the looks of her last text he's up and doing much better."

"Doing better, what she means he's doing much better? And if you were here you wouldn't have to be updated on his health," Scales said with some bass in his voice.

"Look lil nicca, first off, take that bass out when you are talking to me. You must've forgotten who runs this shit and second, I said he's doing much better because Ecstasy told me that Brick keeps grabbing her ass and asking for kisses and shit. Thirdly, nicca, I'm down on the eastside checking up on my other partner DP who might be in trouble. So, you can get your crybaby ass off my phone with that bull shit," Butter said as he hung up his phone.

Scales was just sitting in his car looking at the phone go silent when he remembered Butter wanted all their location turned on. Scales went to the settings in his phone and type Butter number in under location. "Bingo," was all he said as he started up his car and took off.

*   *   *

"DP, thank you for all you have done, I really do appreciate it, but if you know what's best for you, you'll pack your shit and high tail it up out of here. Being around me is like chasing a death wish and no good can come from it. I beg of you just leave. DP just go," Shelly said as she snatched her bloody hands away from him causing spatter blood to go all over the car.

Not trying to hear a word Shelly was saying DP reached back over and took both her hands in his once again. "Listen Shelly, and God dammit you better listen to me good."

This time when he spoke you can hear the love, the caring, the concern, the pain, the strength, the protection, the security you can hear the man who was sent to her. "I'm not going anywhere unless it's in your arms or to run you some bath water or prepare your favorite dish. Shelly since I first laid eyes on you I knew then it's nothing in this world I wouldn't do for you. I'll swim a shark filled ocean to get to you, I'll put my life on the line just to make sure you're

153

safe. What I'm trying to tell you…" DP took one of his blood-stained hands and gently placed it on her chin and turned her face to his. "Is Shelly, I love you and there's nothing I wouldn't do for you."

Hearing this caused Shelly's tears to fall even more and speed up her heart beat. The look in DP's face caused Shelly's panties to get wet between her legs. "DP, I don't know…"

Before she could finish her words, DP placed his mouth on hers and parted her lips with his tongue as they passionately kissed. When they came up for air, Shelly looked DP in the eyes, "DP I love you too."

*   *   *

Scales made it to the beach house in no time. He was dressed in all black with a black hoodie on and a high point black 9-millimeter handgun on his waist line. Now the question he asked himself was how the hell was he going to get in this big ass house undetected with no help to get rid of Butter and DP.

"Ok Butter, you want to talk all that shit, huh? Well, yo time is up. Once you're out the way Brick and the rest of the team wouldn't have a choice but to fall under my leadership or hit the road jack and don't come back no more." Scales laughed to himself as he thought about the movie, 'What's love got to do with it' with Ike and Tina and Ike made Tina eat the cake.

"Hahaha, it's time to make these motherfuckers eat the cake," Scales said as he was having a lil hard time cocking the 9-millimeter handgun. After a few attempts the bullet finally slid in the chamber. Scales looked around to make sure that no one was peeping at his activity when he saw two figures creeping around.

Scales got close enough to the two figures to hear one of them say, "Bum rush the house and kill everything in it." And Scales decided to use this to his advantage.

"Don't move motherfuckers or Imma let loose. Now it's time to play, let's make a deal," Scales said as he removed his hoodie off his head.

*   *   *

"Fuck! See Arsenal, messing around with you this funny looking dude got the drops on us," Clips said not wanting to make any sudden moves to spook the all black assassin.

Arsenal high off cocaine was feeling himself a little too much. "Nicca, do you know who the fuck I am? I'm Arsenal the boss over the T-Y-L click and you got the balls to pull that bullshit gun on me? Nicca 1 should crack yo goddamn head." Arsenal told the assassin as he watched him remove his head wear.

*   *   *

"I see at least one of you clowns can follow direction." Scales told the two he got at gunpoint.

"Nicca I don't follow no fucking directions, you just happened to get the drop on me because I got caught slipping for fucking around with this dope head," Clips said to the nicca who had him at gunpoint.

"Dopehead? Dopehead, nicca I'm Arsenal the leader of the…"

155

Before he could finish Clips cut him off, "Bah, bah, bah nicca don't nobody wanna keep hearing that shit. I'm Arsenal, the leader, bullshit because you're the reason ol'boy got the drop on me."

Arsenal wiped his nose with the back of his hand before he spoke. "You little piece of shit, when we make it out of this situation Imma stick my foot so far up yo' ass, you gonna have Nike prints on the tissue every time you wipe your ass after you take a shit. You hear me little motherfucker?" Clips was about to respond until the assassin who got the drop on them cut him off.

"I wish you or anybody else will try and…"

Tired of hearing the two bickering back and forth, the one unknown man out of the three butt in. "Yo, y'all kill that noise because where I'm standing it's a win, win situation for you playa's."

"How do you figure playa?" Arsenal questioned with some sarcasm in his voice.

The third party out the bunch looked at Arsenal then to Clips. "Because it's oblivious that the three of us are here for a reason."

"Our reasons might be different for yours my guy," Clips said while waving his hand between him and Arsenal.

"Yeah, it might be different," Arsenal said agreeing with Clips as he tried to get one last bump of cocaine out of the plastic baggy. Not able to get any coke up his nose, Arsenal took the cocaine baggy and rubbed it all around the inside of his mouth.

Losing time, the unknown hitman decided to come clean. "Look!"

*   *   *

156

Shelly and DP were on the couch in her living room in front of the fireplace hugged up but not speaking when Shelly spoke first.

"DP?"

"Yes baby."

"I'm so glad that you're here with me but there's a lot you don't know about me and I really don't know how I can explain it to you. You see DP baby I'm…"

As soon as Shelly was about to come clean she was stopped by DP. "Sheesh, listen Shelly, you can save all your confessions for the priest on Sunday because as you can see this here…" DP held up his hands to demonstrate the huge living room to what he was saying. "This here is not the church and I'm not a pastor, but I can lay my hands on your fine ass," DP said as he got playful, rubbing, grabbing, and pinching all over Shelly's body.

"Awww, DP stop!" Shelly said as she laughed and tried to get away from DP's wandering hands.

"Hahaha ok baby that's enough you know I'm ticklish hahaha." Shelly screamed out as DP planted wet kisses all over her face. "OK baby, baby ok you are too much. I'm about to go get in the shower while you make us some drinks," Shelly said as she grabbed him by his ears to bring his face to hers to give him a long passionate kiss.

"Ok sexy, drinks coming right up, but I'm gonna let you know if you keep kissing me like that drinks are going to have to wait because I'll be jumping in that shower with you right now," DP said as he tried to grab Shelly's butt as she pushed his hands away laughing and ran upstairs to the shower.

"Hahaha."

*   *   *
157

"Look!" The unknown hitman said with some irritation in his voice. Clips and Arsenal watched him remove his hoodie to reveal himself. "I'm Scales and it seems like we all are here for a reason. Now the way I see it, we can all help each other and once all parties' affairs are done then we can split and go our separate ways or else?"

"Or else what?" Clips asked not wanting to be the one to bite his tongue.

Scales looked to him and then to Arsenal. "Or else we can start this party now and hope we all have bullets left when the other guests arrive," Scales said as he pointed at the beach house.

Arsenal and Clips both knew he was right. "Fuck it, the bitch Mz. Shell is mine," Arsenal said as he stuck his tongue inside the coke baggy and spit it out his mouth.

*   *   *

Butter sat in his car in front of the beach house continually dialing DP's cellphone which he was still not able to get an answer to. "Shit, Shit still no answer," Butter said as he threw his cellphone down on the passenger seat and decided to go right to the front door of the beach house.

As he's making his way up to the door Butter realized he forgot his pistol back in the car. "Shit, my damn gun." Butter shouted as he descended the stairs two at a time to reach the bottom fast. Butter made it back to his car and noticed the inside light still hasn't gone off yet. *"What the fuck?"* Butter said to himself as he went around to the car to check all the car doors and he noticed that his front passenger door was ajar.

As he looked through the window of the passenger door he saw that his gun wasn't where it should've been. "Ah hell nawl, I know a motherfucker didn't," Butter said as he reached for the handle on the car door. Butter snatched the door open and rampaged the front seats still not able to find his gun. Out of frustration he slammed the car door so hard the window cracked. As he's examining the cracks in the window a person appears behind Butter. If you look through the crack window it seems like plenty of men were behind Butter instead of just one.

Butter seeing this spun around so fast on his heels to look the dude face to face. "Man, who the fuck are you and where the fuck is my pistol."

Chapter 27

"You have a good one," the Uber driver said as he drove away. The stranger had the Uber driver drop him off at a house up the street from the house he was going to. As he rounded the corner he spotted the address to the house he was looking for.

As he's approaching the beach house he sees some random guy exit his vehicle and head upstairs to the beach house. Out of sight, the stranger made his way to the car he saw the guy exit from where he came up on a handgun.

"Damn, I see people just leave all types of things in their car nowadays. And have the nerve to not lock the doors..." the stranger thought to himself as he was rumbling throughout the guy's car. He was getting ready to pop the trunk when he saw him out of the corner of his eye. *"Must've figured out he forgot his pistol..."* the stranger said to himself out loud as he squatted in some nearby bushes. He watched the guy slam his car door and crack the passenger side window, when the stranger decided to pop out.

*   *   *

"Yo?"

"Man, who the fuck are you and where the fuck is my pistol?"

"First things first youngin, who are you and why are you creeping around my people's residence?"

Butter looked at the stranger like he was going mad. "Creeping? Let's not talk because you didn't have a problem creeping around my shit," Butter said to the stranger while pointing at his car.

Getting tired of the back and forth games the stranger raised the gun at Butter, "Talk youngin, and talk fast."

"Damn, then have the balls to point my own shit at me."

"Talk youngin," the stranger said one more time as he cocked Butter's pistol right in his face.

Butter seeing the look in the stranger's face knew he was for real about getting his answer. "Ok, chill old head, I'm just down here trying to locate one of my partners," Butter said holding his hands up as he pleaded with the stranger.

"Partner? Ok, who's your partner that you are referring to?"

"Maybe if you lower 'my' pistol we can come to some agreement."

"Youngin I asked who the fuck are you talking about."

"My partner's name is DP, and about whose house is this I don't know. All I know is I tracked him here to this location and yo ass popped up out of nowhere," Butter said to the stranger.

Hearing this the stranger broke out laughing. "Hahaha."

"Yo, what's funny old head?" Butter wanted to know the butt of the joke and make sure he wasn't it.

The stranger, starting to feel a little relaxed bring the gun down so it wasn't pointed at Butter. "I was laughing youngin, because I normally don't forget information or faces and if I am correct you are Butter."

"Man, how the fuck you know me or my name?"

"No time for answers youngin, but DP and my sista are going to need help soon," the stranger said as he extended his arm out to give Butter back his gun.

"Thanks bro, but you still not telling me who the fuck are you," Butter said as he grabbed his gun back and put it in his waistline.

"Oh yeah, the name is FP, and Shelly is my little sister; and DP is a close partner of mine so let's move," FP said as he dipped off into the night with Butter right behind him.

"Yo, wait up old head, FP or whatever your name is.

*   *   *

Shelly came out of the shower feeling clean and in love, but at the same time down and out about Vest. She just knew sooner than later she was gonna have to get up there to Waupun prison to talk with her brother because he might have some insight on what's going on in the streets from behind the jail cell. You know they say, before they hit the streets the niccas in jail know.

Shelly was in the huge kitchen making her and DP a little snack when DP came up behind her and wrapped his strong arms around her soft, but small waist and gave her a peck on the cheek. "Hey baby, just came in here to check on you and make sure you're doing ok," DP said as he gave her a squeeze of the arms, but not too strong to hurt Shelly.

"Hey baby, just in here fixing us a bite to eat." Only wearing panties and a bra under her robe. Shelly could feel

162

DP's manhood coming alive as it rubbed up against her voluptuous ass.

"That sounds good baby, then after that how about some birthday cake," he said while grabbing a handful of Shelly's butt.

Shelly just laughed and couldn't believe that DP had her blushing like a schoolgirl and she was loving every bit of it.

"How about after you eat you find your way to the shower mister then we can talk about some birthday cake." Shelly told DP as she playfully swatted him on the butt with the dish rag as he ran out the kitchen laughing heading towards the shower.

*   *   *

Scales and the two T-Y-L members found an unlocked window to the garage that led into the beach house. The three were crouched down in the garage with only one door stopping them from entering the house. When Arsenal was one of the first to say something.

"Yo, this the plan, we are just going to kick in that door and everything that moves we are putting bullets in. so let's move on my time," Arsenal said while using the back of his hand to wipe his running nose and using the other hand to point at the door he was referring to.

Clips and scales looked at Arsenal then at themselves and they both gave out a small quiet laugh.

Arsenal didn't take kindly to this. "Yo, what the fuck is funny?" He asked while still wiping his nose because it was still running from the years of cocaine abuse.

"Listen playboy, that there is a janitor closet and that door is the one to the house," Scales said using his gun to

163

demonstrate which door he was talking about. "And far as going in there on some cowboy shit is out of the question."

"So, what do you suggest mister know it all?" Arsenal questioned, getting irritated with not doing nothing at all but crouching in the garage.

"First off, we got to figure out how many people are in this motherfucker," Clips said while checking his guns.

"Nicca, when I want your advice, I'll ask you for it, until then shut the fuck up." Arsenal told Clips.

Clips getting fed up with Arsenal's his mouth was about to go off when Scales butted in. "Yo, kill that noise old head and figure that shit out."

The three sat there for a second thinking about their next move. While Arsenal and Scales, were talking amongst themselves, Clips was off thinking to himself… *"Man, this hoe ass nicca Arsenal always running his mouth. Truth be told he's the reason we're in this shit. Look at him a fucking junkie, a damn coke head. I know one thing: I'm not putting my life on the line for his dope fiend ass no more. As soon as the smoke is clear, I'm out. Let's see how far he get without me ol' dope head ass nicca, talking about running into the janitor closet."* Clips had a smirk on his face.

*   *   *

Butter and FP were going around the beach house trying to find a way in when they ended up back where they started, at Butter's car.

"Damn, it seems like we've been going around this big ass house for hours and still haven't found a crack door, window, nothing that will get us in this motherfucker,"

Butter said bent over with both his hands on his hips gasping for air.

"I hear ya youngin, but it gotta be a way to get in. Aye, how were you going to get in before I came along?" FP asked Butter who was just now getting his breath back.

"Whew shit, I need to get in somebody's gym but I was just going to ring the doorbell and ask who came to the door, was DP in there, shit that's how."

They both gave out a laugh when FP said, "Fuck it let's try that way then." And they both was on their way up the stairs to ring the doorbell.

*   *   *

Shelly and DP were laid up in the master bedroom watching reruns of 'Wild-N-Out.' DP's head rested on Shelly's stomach as she ran her fingers through his hair while he dozed off to her touch. Shelly was full and was just about to join DP with his nap when she set up in bed because she thought she heard a noise. This certain movement out the blue startled DP and had him wondering what was going on.

"Baby are you ok, what's wrong?" DP asked Shelly as he looked around the master bedroom trying to figure out if they were safe.

"I don't know baby, I thought I heard a noise coming from somewhere in the house but I might be tripping."

Not taking any chances DP got right up to investigate with Shelly on his heels. They made it to the stairs that led downstairs. Soon as they made it to the bottom of the stairs they heard the doorbell ring and someone banging on the door screaming DP's name.

"Ding dong, ding dong, Bam, Bam. DP it's me, Butter the little homie, you in this bitch or what? DP!!!"

DP and Shelly both looked at each other with a what the fuck look on their face as they both said, "Butter!" at the same time.

*   *   *

When the three stowaways in the garage heard all the commotion they figured this was the best time to try.

"Yo let's do this," Scales said as he reached for the door knob that led into the house and found it to be unlocked.

While Scales and Arsenal were making their way into the main parts of the house, Clips was heading the opposite direction on his way out the house. *"Man fuck Arsenal and that other nicca from this point on, I'm a loner,"* Clips said to himself as he left the beach house garage the same way he came in.

As Arsenal and Scales are making their way through out the house, Scales turned around and didn't see Clips. "Aye, yo' old head"

"What nicca, don't you see me getting ready to handle business, why the fuck are you yo'ing me?"

"I don't see your young boy Clips anywhere, where the fuck do you think he went?" Scales asked Arsenal with a hush tone in his voice.

"What, where did the fucker go?"

"Hell, I don't know, that's why I was yo'ing you nicca." Scales told him while thinking to himself... *"Man this nicca is doped out, I should've left with the youngin fucked around and get off fucking with his fiend ass, damn."*

Arsenal turned to Scales, "Man fuck that nicca, I'll deal with his snake ass later," he said as he rounded a corner that led to the front living room with Scales right behind him on alert with a bad feeling in his gut.

*   *   *

"Go ahead and ring that bell, beat or kick on the door, do whatever you have to do to get their asses to the door. I'm gonna stand over here in the cut and make sure no one gets a chance to sneak up on us like I did you," FP said with a smirk on his face as he stepped to the side out the way and unnoticeable.

"Very funny nicca, I forgot to laugh, ha motherfucker ha," Butter said as he rang the doorbell, banged on the door and screamed DP's name. "Yo' DP!!"

Hearing it was Butter calling his name DP crept to the door more relaxed. When he made it to the big oak wood door he yelled out Butter's name. "Butter is that you?"

"Yeah DP it's me, now open the door and stop playing because we got to talk. There's a lot of strange shit going on. Like why are you at Shelly's house, y'all two are a couple now, shit I can't blame you, she is fine..."

Right before Butter finished the big doors swung open. "Butter get yo' ass in here," DP said as he snatched Butter by his shirt and pulled him in.

"Damn big homie, be easy, the shirt cost me a few bands, not to mention all the bullshit I've been going through the last few days," Butter said as he walked past Shelly and DP and flopped down on Shelly's *$12,000* one-piece Ashley couch.

"Well, join the party because we haven't been having a cake walk," Shelly said as she tightened up her robe.

"Trust me boss lady, I know y'all haven't, I seen how y'all two tore out the parking lot, that's how I got here it took me a while trying to figure out how to get in this nice ass beach house. When it dawns on me, fuck it just ring the doorbell but first I had to persuade y'all homeboy, matter of fact where the fuck did he go?" Butter asked as he looked past Shelly and DP.

Hearing Butter was with somebody else got DP and Shelly on pins and needles. Shelly rushed to the door and double locked them while DP questioned Butter. "Butter you said my homeboy, who were you talking about?"

Butter looked at them like they were crazy. "DP stop playing big homie, you know who I am talking about."

Just before Butter could get the words out of his mouth Arsenal and Scales rounded the corner.

*　　　*　　　*

"So, what the fuck do we have here?" Arsenal asked out loud as him and Scales rounded the corner that led into the living room where the intended hosts were at.

Scales seeing Butter on the couch with this shocked look on his face only enraged him. "Talk yo shit now nicca."

*　　　*　　　*

"Talk that shit now nicca," Scales said to Butter as he slapped him in the face with the butt of his gun.

"Aww, what the fuck, you snake ass nicca. All the shit I have done for your ass, when I get out of here I'm gonna personally…"

"Bam!" Scales slapped Butter again across the top of his head cracking it like an uncooked egg. Instead of yellow egg yolk coming out of Butter's head it was a bright red thick bloody liquid that poured out of his head onto Shelly's expensive furniture.

"Oh you motherfuckers!" Butter yelled out as he dropped to his knees and used his hand to cover up his eyes so that the blood wouldn't get in them and blind him. The way Butter yelled out motherfuckers it seemed like he was trying to mock the famous actor Denzel Washington in the hit movie 'Training Day.'

Seeing this unfold, DP positioned Shelly in back of him. Arsenal was enjoying the show until he saw Shelly moving. "Uh uh Mz. Shelly don't you go about all that moving now. Even though Big Vest is no longer with us, I still don't trust yo ass or the baby Vest nicca you got with you. So how about you do me a favor and move your pretty ass right back in front of the baby Vest nicca if you kindly don't mind," Arsenal said.

Shelly knew that Arsenal was a junkie and would shoot anything and anybody when he's off drugs. "Ok Arsenal, I'm stepping around him just take it easy," Shelly said as she made her way around DP.

Scales seeing Butter drop to his knees brought a sense of power over him. "Ok big dawg, it's time you get what's coming to you." Scales told DP as he raised his gun in his direction.

Now at this point, DP and Shelly were side by side. When Shelly stepped back from behind DP she let her robe come undone on purpose.

"DP baby, don't you wish you could have a piece of this birthday cake right now because baby it's all yours, so grab it like you want it." Shelly told DP. DP looked down at Shelly's butt and he could see the .380 she had strapped to her back.

"Damn, I love her but we are going to have to talk if we ever get out of this shit." DP thought to himself.

"Ok DP time to meet your maker, and Butter yo bitch ass is next," Scales said as he squeezed the trigger on the high point blue steel nine.

"Click, click." Nothing, "Cheap as bullshit high point," Scales said as he tried to unjam his weapon.

Those two hits to Butter's face and skull was all it took to malfunction the high point .9. Not giving Scales a chance to unjam his weapon, DP reached down behind Shelly's back and came up with the .380 firing.

"Boom, boom, boom, boom."

DP fired four times and three of the bullets found their way inside Scales upper body killing him on the spot. Arsenal was so coked up when DP got to firing he thought he was the one letting off the shots until Scales fell into him causing his gun to fall out of his hand.

Arsenal was about to turn and leave so he could fight his battle another day but was stopped cold in his tracks by something cold against the back of his head.

"Going somewhere so soon?" The stranger asked Arsenal as he stepped in his view so he could get a peek of the person who snuck up behind him and got the drop on him.

"Say man who the fuck are you? My beef is with her and her alone. Not you or any of these other motherfuckers, just her."

"I don't know who either one of you niccas are but to get to her, you motherfuckers are going to have to get through me. And y'all can bet your last dollar I don't move easily," DP said as he positioned Shelly back behind him with the .380 still raised in the air.

"DP chill lil-bro I got it from here." Hearing that voice, it sounded so familiar to DP.

"Fam, do I know you?" DP asked the stranger.

"I told you it's your homeboy the whole damn time," Butter said as he took off his shirt to try and wipe the blood out of his eyes.

"No, it can't be, it just can't be," Shelly said as she tightened back up her robe. DP gun hand started to come down and a smile started to appear on his face.

"Arsenal, your beef has always been with me, you just didn't know it," the stranger said as he took the hoodie off his head.

"FP!" As Arsenal said his name a bullet was leaving the gun FP had and finding his way inside Arsenal, killing him standing up.

FP turned around with a smile on his face. "I can't get a hug from my baby sister or homeboy?" As he stood there with his arms stretched out with a smile on his face that said... IM HOME!!

Chapter 28

"By the power invested in me, I pronounce you husband and wife, you may kiss the bride now," the pastor said to the now married couple. DP lifted up Shelly's veil and gave her a passionate kiss a husband could give his new wife.

DP, FP and Butter were all at the bar at the reception having drinks enjoying themselves.

"Congrats big homie, I wish you and boss lady, who I love like a sister nothing but the best in the world," Butter said as the three toasted and downed a shot.

"Same here lil bro, I hope you and my baby sister live a long productive happy life," FP said as the three toast another shot of liquor.

"Man, I just want you both to know I wouldn't be here without y'all and together we are going to get this money on a whole new level. I love you man," DP said as the three took one more shot.

"Well, boys it's a lot of single women here so it's about time I make my rounds," Butter said just as he was getting ready to make his rounds Brick came on the mic.

"I just asked Ecstasy to marry me and she said Yes!"

Butter turned to DP and FP, "Shit I better move fast," and was gone in the crowd.

"FP, I want to thank you for getting my bread from that crook ass lawyer. I really don't know how to thank you," DP said as he took a sip of his Bud Light beer.

"No thanks needed my brother. Just make sure you keep that smile on her face," FP said just as Shelly was walking up.

"No problem FP, no problem."

Shelly came up wobbling because she was six months pregnant with twins. "Baby did you hear the good news?" Brick proposed to Ecstasy and she said yes. Me and her have so much work to do, first we need to…"

"Baby what do you mean, y'all have so much to do?" DP asked his new wife.

"Baby she asked me to help her plan it."

"On that note, I think I'll catch up with Butter," FP said laughing as he walked away.

"What is he laughing at?" Shelly asked her new husband.

"Nothing baby, you just make sure you get some rest and feed my two boys or girls or boy and girl," DP said as he planted kisses on his pregnant wife's stomach.

"I love you DP."

"I love you more Mz. Shelly." They both laughed and shared a husband and wife kiss.

*   *   *

- On The East Side of Town -

It's been almost two years since the reign and terror of the T-Y-L crew has come to an end. Clips set in his Cutlass with an up and coming thug, who went by the name Lil BP.

"Yo youngster, I've been hearing your name getting a buzz down here on the East side and I must say, I'm liking what I've been hearing." Clips told the younger one out of them.

"You know, big dawg, it's nothing. A gangster like myself, just trying to survive in this jungle with these Lions, Apes and Bears. Shit, they call me the zookeeper with this big bad motherfucker right here," Lil BP said as he held up his mini sized Drake-o, like it was on display at a talent show.

"See my nicca, that's why I like you. You stay ready so you don't have to get ready. You know just like I know in these streets only the strong survive, dog eat dog feel me G?" Clips tested as he passed the blunt of Za that they were smoking on.

"Yeah, both of my ears are working so I most definitely hear ya' big dawg, but feeling you, I don't know about that just yet," Lil BP said while passing Clips back the blunt of Za.

Clips hit the Za a few more times then sat it back in the ashtray and turned towards Lil BP. "Dig this lil homie, it's my turn to run these mean streets of MIlwaukee. So, I'm giving yo young ass the opportunity to get down with the nicca who is going to be wearing the crown, me. The soon to be King. So, while you're thinking about it, run yo lil ass in that store and grab me a bag of chips and pack of smokes, lil thinking ass nicca." Lil BP got out and closed the door. He took three steps towards the store and turned around.

Clips at first wasn't paying Lil BP any attention because he had a quick reminiscence about Baby Nine. *"Damn, Baby Nine, wish you were here and us together would've had this city on lock."* Clips came out of his thoughts to Lil BP staring through the passenger window.

"Yo, you get my shit?" He asked Lil BP who was at the car door with a smile on his face.

"Nawl OG, you never told me what kind of smokes you wanted."

Clips smiled at Lil BP and said, "See, that's why you'll make a good addition to my crew because if you don't know something you are supposed to ask questions. Newport shorts Lil BP and don't forget my damn chips."

Lil BP said, "Bet Clips and I made my decision."

"So, what did you come up with?" Clips asked him as he reached back into the ashtray and retrieved the blunt of Za they were smoking on.

Lil BP looked at Clips. "What I came up with is this…" Clips turned and looked at Lil BP who came up with the mini sized Drake-O.

"Snake ass nicca, I came up with this and a few more reasons why I'm not fucking with no has been T-Y-L member." Lil BP pulled the trigger on the mini sized assault rifle which released three bullets at once. The assault rifle was so accurate that all three bullets found the exact mark in Clips neck that his head was almost decapitated from his body.

Lil BP reached in the car and grabbed the still smoking blunt out of Clips hand and was gone like a thief in the night. "I'll take that bitch ass, snake ass nicca."

*   *   *

- Few hours later back at the reception -

Brick, FP and DP were sitting at the bar poolside having drinks enjoying each other's company.

"So, Bricks, you ready to take that leap into marriage huh?" DP asked him.

"Yeah, big homie, it's about time plus, Ecstasy is the one for me because through the good and the bad, she

175

always had my back," Brick said, as he took a sip of his beer and stared at his future wife on the other side of the pool who was all smiles and laughs with Shelly and the rest of the bridesmaids and women.

"Well, to that Brick, we salute you with love and respect, power and wealth," FP said as he took a drink of his Hennessy.

"Damn you boys having drinks without me?" Butter walked up and grabbed a bottle of Moet Rose Champagne out of a bucket of ice that was on chill.

"We were wondering, where you went to Butter?" DP asked him as he lit him up a cigarette.

"DP you know me, I was introducing myself to some of those fine ass bridesmaids over there, when I ran into this lil nicca here." The other three friends looked up to see LIl BP.

"Oh, shit it's the lil homie Lil BP, what's up kid?" They all said as they gave him a dap and the man hug. After some time, the other men got to mingling amongst other guests while FP and Lil BP were left alone at the bar.

"So, did you take care of that BP?"

"Come on Unc, you know I took care of that so-called situation, that nicca is in hell getting his ass whooped by my pop's right now as we speak." Just when FP was about to say something Shelly walked up.

"Well, if it isn't my nephew Lil BulletProof, I'm so glad you could make it," she said as she gave him a hug and a kiss on the cheek.

"Come on Auntie, you know I wouldn't miss this for the world," Lil BulletProof told her back.

"Well, let me get back to my guest before I get to crying, seeing my nephew and my brother here sitting together," Shelly said as she went back to entertain her guest.

FP and Lil BP both had smiles on their faces as Shelly walked away.

"Yeah, Tete has always been like that. Haha, so Unc, what's your plans now that you are a free man?" Lil BP asked FP as he lit the same blunt back up that he took out of Clip's hand.

"First off Lil BP, I want you to know that your daddy Big Vest would've been so proud of you right now, just like I am, how you got revenge for his death. And nephew, about the question you asked me. I'm going to need your help."

"My help Unc, what you need done, you know I'm with the smoke."

"Naw nephew, it's about we switch the game."

"Well, don't keep him in the dark, tell the youngster what is the next move." Lil BulletProof looked up to see DP, Brick and Butter around him.

"Well, like I was saying, we are about to start a nonprofit charitable organization called: P.P.T.G.D.P which stands for, Please Put The Guns Down People.

THE END

Acknowledgements

I would like to thank my brother from another mother, CEO Author Kendrick Watkins. Who stayed on me and helped me stay focused on the big road ahead and more thanks to the team at S.Y.C.W.P it's all love. And tto all the fans who love S.Y.C.W.P's books, we thank you all for the love and support from your's truly…

Author Deyon Lee
B.K.A
Mr. Flock!

But on a more serious note, this book is all fiction but P.P.T.G.D.P could be a real thing with the help of each and every one.

Please. Put. The. Guns. Down. Please

SO YOU CAN WRITE
PUBLICATIONS®

www.sycwp.com
"Where the writers go…"

www.ingramcontent.com/pod-product-compliance
Lightning Source LLC
Chambersburg PA
CBHW020227030726
47497CB00009B/2989